ROCKET SCIENCE

Rocket Science

JEANNE WILLIS

ff

faber and faber

First published in 2002
by Faber and Faber Limited
3 Queen Square London WC1N 3AU

Typeset by Faber and Faber
Printed in England by Mackays of Chatham plc, Chatham, Kent

A CIP record for this book
is available from the British Library

ISBN 0–571–21275–1

2 4 6 8 10 9 7 5 3 1

For Edward
With special thanks to Graham Morris, without whom the
rocket would never have got off the ground.
Also to Shirley Rose for her help and advice.

West of these out to seas colder than the Hebrides I must go
Where the fleet of stars is anchored and the young
star-captains glow.

James Elroy Flecker 1884–1917

Chapter One

'Repeat after me, Dweeb. Jesus died so I could ride.'

Sonny had Adam in a stranglehold. He could hardly breathe, let alone repeat anything. It didn't bother him much. It was one of many unprovoked attacks; he was quite used to them.

It had become a game of endurance. As a rule, he looked forward to the cartoon-like moments when Sonny would pounce on him. Yes, it hurt, but the pain was nothing compared to the rush of pleasure he got from refusing to struggle. It spoilt all Sonny's fun.

'Fight back, Dweeb!'

'La, la, la, la, la.'

Today, he could have done without the interruption. He'd been trying to concentrate on the opening sentence of a book Uncle Eugene had lent him:

The earth is an insignificant dot against the
overwhelming backcloth of space.

Whoah! The notion had blown his mind.

The earth is an insignificant dot . . .

He was lost in thought. He was in a galaxy far, far away. He was on the brink of understanding the meaning of the universe when Sonny marched in, snatched the book and told him it was his turn to clean out the python. Adam blinked at him slowly, as if he'd made an idiotic mistake.

'I did it last week. You do it.'

Instinctively, Sonny put his two brain cells together and

attacked him. It was so inevitable it was laughable. Oh, here we go again . . .

'*Repeat after me, Dweeb* . . . '

Adam smiled and remained wilfully silent throughout the entire episode apart from a few unavoidable gurgles. There would have been less chance of having his throat squeezed if he'd agreed to clean out the python, but where was the fun in that? It was Sonny's turn. He knew Sonny was scared and that pleased him no end.

It was a pretty big snake. After it had eaten a rat, it was the width of a full toilet roll. His dad, Chas, had inherited it from Grandad Clem who used to keep it in his tattoo parlour. It was very docile but Adam noticed that Sonny broke out in a sweat whenever it was at large. Right now, it was oozing round its vivarium, looking forward to lunch.

Sonny tightened his grip. His hands stank of motorbike grease.

'I'm going down to the yard to work on Baby,' he hissed. 'When I come back, the python will be all clean and shiny . . . *won't it?*'

Baby was a motorbike – a Harley FXRT. Chas had bought it second-hand from a retired Hell's Angel called Skunk. When he wasn't serving in the shop, he was going to help Sonny strip it down. By the time they'd finished, Baby would look as mean as the machine Chas used to ride when he was a member of The Hung Priests.

Sonny loved his bike more than any girl he'd ever known – and he'd known plenty. 'She's going to have high bars and a teardrop gas tank and a skinny front wheel and a bitch bar,' he said. 'Not that *you'd* understand, Dweeb.'

Adam did understand. He'd spent most of his childhood parked in the workshop at the back of Lurie's Motors. He'd seen so many engines stripped down he could build his own bike if the mood took him. Only he wasn't interested. His father took it as a personal insult.

'How come you haven't got petrol in your veins, like

Sonny? Biking's in your blood. Your mum even rode with the Angels.'

She wasn't in the saddle for long though. Adam's mother was only sixteen when she ran off with his father. He was ten years older than her. Next spring, Sonny was born, Apple of Chas's eye, fruit of his leathery old loins. Poor Karen. Her hell-raising days were over.

After Sonny started school , she'd set her heart on going to college but to her everlasting disappointment, found she was expecting Adam. She had to stay right where she was – wiping bums, doing the books, serving in the motorbike shop.

And where was she now, while he was being strangled? Taking his little sister Fay to ballet. Or was it violin? Or pony club? Or kung fu? Spoilt little brat. Just as Adam's windpipe was about to close up, Sonny got bored and let go. Grinning horribly, he scooped up a handful of *Star Wars* figures Adam had arranged on the window sill. He chose one and dangled it out of the window.

'Now, ask yourself. Are you going to get off your spotty, white arse and do as I tell you? Or do I have to send Puke Skywalker into the overwhelming backcloth of space? Oh! I wonder if he can fly?'

Having got the attention he craved, Sonny opened his thumb and finger and Luke Skywalker plummeted onto the pavement two storeys below.

Adam's mouth fell open. The act of deliberately and maliciously dropping Luke Skywalker had caught him off-guard. He was finding it very difficult to pretend he didn't care. An aeroplane went by. Sonny cupped his hand to his ear.

'Hark . . . that'll be Daft Vader come to finish him off.'

Something in Adam snapped.

'Idiot! 'he yelled. 'Stupid, thick gorilla!'

Sonny was delighted to have prompted such a strong reaction for once. Adam was furious with himself for revealing his weak spot. For a moment, he wasn't sure what to do. His strategy of non-retaliation had failed. Yet he had to act

[3]

quickly to knock the satisfied smirk off Sonny's face. He bent over to pick up the book Uncle Eugene had lent him and hurled it with as much violence as he could muster, hoping to hit Sonny between his eyes. Fortunately, he was a lousy shot. The book clumped his brother right between the legs and he collapsed on the carpet in a whimpering heap. It was hard to tell who was the most surprised. While Sonny was busy getting the dent out of his testicles, Adam revelled in his victory for a few glorious seconds.

'Ha! Got you in the brain!'

Then he legged it out of the flat, down the stairs and through the shop where his father was fixing a puncture on his uncle's ancient push-bike. Uncle Eugene called after him:

'Adam! That book I lent you on Interstellar Space Flight. Not too heavy, was it?'

'It was for Sonny! Sorry, can't stop, I'm running away from home.'

His dad didn't even look up.

'What, again? Good for you!' called Uncle Eugene. 'Run like the wind!'

Adam ran backwards, waving with one hand and sticking two fingers up at Sonny, who was pointing an air rifle at him from the upstairs window. No way was that thing loaded.

Bang!

It was just a car backfiring. Probably. Even so, Adam hurled himself dramatically round the corner and taking Uncle Eugene's advice, ran as fast as a boy can run when someone's trying to shoot him in cold blood.

Adam didn't stop running until he came to the cliff path. It was about midday, but there was no one around. There never was. This part of the coast wasn't popular with the locals, let alone the tourists. The cliff path was overgrown and steep. There were no steps. Even if you did make it to the bottom, it was all shingle and sandflies – hardly picture-postcard material. But he liked it. It was his secret place.

The only other person who knew about it was Moses. They

used to go there after school and make camps in the caves. There was a favourite cave which could only be entered by crawling through a small hole, overhung by scrubby gorse. They'd found it by accident, or, rather, Moses had. He'd been trying to entice a baby seagull down from a ledge with a length of liquorice when he'd missed his footing, fallen head first into the gorse and found himself staring into a vast cavern.

'Wicked! Come and look at this, Adam!'

It was much bigger than the other caves they'd found. It was bigger than Uncle Eugene's bedsit. There was enough room for the two of them to set up home.

'We could put beds in here, man. We could sleep over!' Moses had said. 'A table. Chairs! We could get one of those oil heaters. Heat it up in the winter. What d'you think?'

'There's no electrics, Moses.'

'Oh, right. I was getting carried away with it being so magnificent. It's like a holy place. A lickle cathedral or something.'

Adam gazed up at the arched ceiling. Millions of years ago, it had been carved into hundreds of gargoyles by the sea. Water dripped over a formation of stone pipes, playing a constant, eerie xylophone. Miniature sparks of daylight shone through the open pores in the rock. Moses was impressed.

'We got indoor stars.'

Theirs were the only footprints in the sand that carpeted the floor. It was easy to believe no other humans had been there before.

Over the Easter holidays, they made the cave their own.

Moses had rigged up a bed out of plastic crates and brought his beanbag along for a mattress. Adam brought an old eiderdown and arranged it on an inflatable lilo in a little alcove. There was a battered kitchen cupboard they'd found in a builder's skip, which they filled with matches, candles, food and batteries. They even had a portable barbecue.

Once inside, they would block the entrance with a piece of driftwood and disappear from the face of the earth.

Adam christened it The Black Hole. They would sit there,

eating cheese and onion crisps, the first astronauts ever to survive the gravitational pull of a collapsed, giant star. In the inky, echoing space of the cave they were a million light years from home. There would be a thoughtful silence, then Moses would pipe up:

'You know Europa, smallest of Jupiter's four largest moons, yeah? Well, on *News at Ten*, this guy, right? He reckons it's got its own ocean.'

Moses was convinced there was life on other planets and the tiniest shred of evidence was seized upon with infectious enthusiasm.

'Won't be long now, man. They're out there, all right. Wonder what they look like? You think like ET?'

Adam had first seen *ET* on video when he was six. It had affected him deeply, penetrating the most sensitive crinkle in his brain. He'd sat slumped on the sofa alone, in a state of shock, gasping for oxygen as the credits rolled, tears spilling into his bowl of popcorn.

It was like a religious calling only without a god. It stirred in him the unshakeable belief that extra-terrestrials existed and that they would walk among us, on Earth. Like a missionary, he would dedicate his life to spreading the word, much to the hilarity of his family and his classmates.

'Seen any little green men lately, Dweeb?'

He couldn't understand why everyone thought the idea was such a joke. He found it insulting and narrow-minded. He didn't mock the Catholic kids for believing in Mary. He'd made a Diwali lamp in pottery in good faith. He'd never snatched the little cap – the kipa – off his Jewish cousin and thrown it over the wall. But for some reason, it was fine to persecute *him*.

It was even worse when he announced he wanted to be an astronaut when he grew up. He was convinced there was no other possible career, but again, people had other ideas.

It upset his father, who wanted him to work in Lurie's Motors selling second-hand motorbikes. It irritated his mother, who groaned and said, 'Oh, God. You'll end up just like Uncle Eugene.' Sonny had to have his say, of course. He reckoned they wouldn't allow Dweebs in space because they were too weedy to survive the gravitational pull. Then he threatened to throw him off the roof to prove it. Even Fay laughed at him.

'You'll look silly in a space helmet,' she said.

The only person who didn't take the mick was Moses.

'Don't take no notice of your family,' he said. 'You know why? Sorry to say it, but get real. They're all fick. You're the clever one. That's how come you don't fit in.'

It made sense. That's why he hadn't fitted in at school either. He'd started off so well. Top grades in everything, except PE. His mathematical skills, they said, were exceptional. His grasp of technical drawing, superb. His IQ, phenomenal.

All of which made him unpopular with his peers. The one lesson Adam failed to grasp at school was that nobody liked a Smart Arse. He could have pretended to be thick to make himself more popular, but he was a poor actor. Most of them couldn't hold an intelligent conversation with him anyway, which is why he tended to talk to himself.

While no one was actively nasty to him, the rest of the class had him down as a small version of the Nutty Professor. The ones who chose to sit next to him only did so because they couldn't finish their homework. That was, until Moses arrived.

He'd joined in Year Five. The only empty seat in the class was next to Adam, so the logical place for the teacher to put him was there. For once, fate was kind. Moses wasn't just clever, he was intuitive. Wise beyond his years. He could sit next to anyone in the room and know how to bring the best out of them.

'You want to be *what*? An astronaut? No kidding, me too!'

Moses had no natural enemies. He rapidly became the most popular boy in the class, but he chose to befriend Adam.

They hit it off immediately. Within a week, Moses' friendship healed the chronic bruise that had been bothering him for most of his life. It was Moses who gave him the strategy for coping with Sonny. It took three simple words:

'Ignore him, man.'

If anyone else had said it, it would have sounded crass. It was the *way* Moses said things. He was a witch doctor with a bag of mantras that made you invincible. Adam tried it and nine times out of ten, it worked.

That last year at school had been bliss. Because Moses was popular and hung around with Adam, Adam suddenly got respect. He didn't like it much when he had to share Moses with the others. He felt uncomfortable larking about in a gang but he did his best to dumb down and join in. It was a small price to pay for a soulmate.

The Friday before Moses emigrated, they bunked off choir practice and spent the whole afternoon in The Black Hole. Moses had given Adam his pewter figurine of Luke Skywalker as a keepsake. Adam gave Moses his Yoda. They'd carved their names on the cave wall with a piece of glass:

Starflight Commander M. Shoderu April 1999
Captain A. Lurie April 1999

Moses was in South Africa now – Cape Town. Adam missed him so much, he felt as if someone had scraped his insides out. He would wake up happy some days, then he'd remember Moses had gone and feel physically ill. He'd try to picture his face, but he couldn't hold it – after a few seconds, it would dissolve into a brown blur, just like it did when they said goodbye.

He tried to remember his voice. It was quite deep and husky. He closed his eyes and played it in his head like a tape. He re-wound it and played it back, but although the words were right, it sounded like a stranger.

'Cape Town ain't far away. Cape Town's just down the

road. You and me? We're going way, way farver than that. In a spaceship, right? For real!'

As Adam climbed the cliff path down to the beach, he remembered an astronomical fact he'd discovered that morning:

'The mean distance from Pluto to the sun is approximately 5916,000,000 kilometres.'

Moses would have got a real buzz from all those kilometres. Getting his head round astronomical distances really turned him on. Now he wasn't around, there was no one else to share the thrill. There was Uncle Eugene, but he was an ex-physics teacher so it took more than a few billion kilometres to get him going. He'd heard it all before.

Adam was looking at six whole weeks with nothing to do and no one to do it with. He stood in the middle of the shingle and shouted at the top of his voice.

'Moses, come back! I need someone to talk to!'

There was no reply. He booted a rusty can across the shingle. It bounced noisily over the pebbles then rolled into the scum at the edge of the tide. He chased after it, kicking it furiously:

'I can't talk to *Sonny* and I can't talk to *Dad* and I can't talk to *Mu* . . .'

He was about to kick it into the water when a retreating wave exposed something large and metallic a little way out to sea.

It submerged again for a few seconds, but as the tide rolled back, the sun bounced sharply off the metal, making him squint. Adam kicked off his trainers, rolled up his trousers and waded in to investigate.

The coldness of the water gripped his ankles and took his breath away. He leapt back on to the shingle and wondered if he should wait for the tide to go out a bit further.

The lure of the unknown treasure was too strong. Somehow, he knew it was a major find. Bracing himself, he paddled slowly over to it.

The waves slapped the back of his knees. Adam already suspected the object was a washed-up engine of some kind – probably an old outboard motor. As he got nearer, he realized with increasing excitement that it was nothing of the sort. He could tell from the fancy-looking rotor that it was part of an engine, but it hadn't fallen off a speedboat – it was too big. Maybe it had fallen off of a jumbo jet!

The rotor was encased in a studded, silver tube, wider than his shoulders and about as high as his chest. There was no rust on it and no barnacles. It couldn't have been there long.

The rest of the tube was buried in the seabed. Quite how deep, he didn't know. Adam pushed against the exposed bulk to see if he could shift it. It wouldn't budge. Maybe he should try rocking it with his whole body to break the suction.

After some difficulty, he found that if he really stretched, he could get his arms round far enough to grip on to a couple of large bolts. Mounting the thing like a pogo stick, his feet supported on two partially exposed fins that stuck out on either side, he began to thrust himself backwards and forwards.

For a while, nothing happened and he felt idiotic. Then he felt a slight shift. At the same time, it crossed his mind he could be clinging to a bomb left over from World War Two. His stomach lurched. In his panic to dismount, his body-weight levered the whole contraption out of its sandy grave. There was a loud suck and he was thrown backwards into the sea.

Spitting salt water out of his mouth and trying to regain his balance on the slippery seaweed, Adam jabbed his leg on the corner of something hard which was bobbing below the surface – it was a studded wooden crate, bound with silver wire. Most of the lid had been smashed away, but the contents were sealed in with an opaque, plastic skin, so he couldn't see what was inside – and there was definitely something inside.

He looked round to make sure the tube with the rotor wasn't about to drift away while he rescued the crate. To his relief, it had been washed up on to the beach and was rolling in a puddle of brine like a stranded shark.

The crate was surprisingly light. Using the wire binding to pull it along, he brought it ashore and slit the plastic seal open with his penknife.

There was a life-sized construction kit inside, a cross between Meccano and Airfix, but Adam had no idea what the finished model was meant to be. There were no instructions.

The biggest part was a silvery white, metal tube. It was almost the width of the crate and had a curved grill. Inside this tube, progressively narrower tubes were stored, each with its own set of bolts and pre-punched holes.

Right at the bottom was a plastic bag, which contained various bits of hardware and a spanner, but still no instructions. He'd just have to work it out for himself.

Adam put his trainers back on and dragged the crate back to his cave. That was the easy bit – the tube with the fins was much more awkward. By the time he'd managed to shuffle and roll it to The Black Hole, his hands were a mass of blisters.

He had to take the fins off to fit the tube into the cave. Luckily, he was able to use the spanner from the crate and managed to remove them without much of a struggle. He put the nuts and bolts in his pocket and was about to shunt the rotor casing into the narrow hole when he heard voices.

No one must see what he'd found! The rush of adrenalin gave him the burst of strength he needed to haul the whole thing inside. With trembling fingers, he dragged the lump of driftwood over the entrance and crouched in silence, hypersensitive to the slightest noise outside.

There was no one there. The voices must have been seagulls. He lit some candles, placed all the metal tubes in a row on the cave floor and arranged the loose fins around the end section. When he'd finished, he sat down and tried to fathom out what it was he'd found.

Several thoughts crossed his mind. This could be part of a

submarine. Maybe even a nuclear submarine. Say it was contaminated with radiation? He'd die a hideous, slow death, then everyone would be sorry – Sonny, for calling him a Dweeb. Dad, for not liking him as much as Sonny. And Fay for being Mum's favourite.

How his mother would weep as he lay in his coffin in his *Star Wars* pyjamas, so young, so talented!

'If only I'd bought him that telescope he wanted instead of wasting money on riding lessons for his sister.'

She'd toss a single, red rose into his grave and Uncle Eugene would have to stop her throwing herself in, crying, 'Why, oh why didn't I spend more time with Adam instead of going to aerobics with my friends?'

As he sat there brushing wet sand from the rotor casing and planning the lavish buffet for his own funeral, he noticed a series of pale, red marks near the base. He spat on the metal and rubbed hard. It was writing of some kind, but he didn't recognize the language.

Maybe it was Russian and this was a stray missile left over from the Cold War. A lot of hardware had gone missing over the years. Stolen and sold to terrorists hell-bent on nuking the Brits, according to Uncle Eugene.

On the other hand, the letters could have been Chinese or Arabic. It was difficult to tell, because the top layer of paint had scratched away.

What he had found might have been just a tiny part of something as big as Concorde. Or it might just be a small thing. It was impossible to tell when he only had part of the jigsaw. He wasn't even sure that the finned tube and the contents of the crate were related.

Adam wondered whether other vital parts might have been washed up further down the coast, but right now, he felt like a tiger with a fresh kill – he wasn't about to abandon it.

Having paced round the sum of the parts two or three times, he decided to view everything from a different angle. Despite his poor PE report, he was an excellent climber and leapt with monkey-like speed onto a rocky ledge near the ceiling.

As he stared down at all the pieces, it suddenly struck him that the tube with the rotor looked exactly like the back end of a rocket!

Once that tantalizing thought had entered his head, it was impossible to shift. The more he looked at it from above, the easier it was to picture how the thing must have looked in its entirety. Now the fins made sense, and the stuff in the crate? The crate must have been on board at some point. It was the kit – or part of the kit – needed to send the rocket back into space!

But where had it come from? America, perhaps? No, if it was American, it would have been covered in logos and adverts for Coke.

Was it something to do with Britain's contribution to the space station, then? They were always losing things. He hadn't heard about it on the news, but they might have kept it from the press for security reasons. Adam was about to climb down none the wiser, when he had a brain-bursting thought which almost made him fall off the ledge.

'Oh . . . oh, it is! It *has* to be!'

His hands were shaking so much he only just managed to adjust the mouthpiece on his imaginary space helmet:

'This is Captain Lurie to Starflight Commander Shoderu. I have an unidentified rocket parked in The Black Hole. Do you think it could have come from another planet? Over.'

He stuffed his fist into his groin and chewed his other knuckle hard to try and calm himself down, but it was impossible. He'd found a rocket. An *alien* rocket!

An echo came back. It was as if Moses had heard him in Cape Town and was delighted to share the good news.

'Y . . . es, Captain Lurie. Ohhhhhh, yes!'

Chapter Two

Adam was busily bolting some of the metal tubes together when he heard voices again. This time, they were real. It was kids. They were close enough for him to make out some of the words.

'Jay! Over here, quick!'

He was furious. They were trespassing on his patch. What were they doing up this end of the bay?

'What ? What've you found? Is it a jellyfish?'

'Just get over here. Get Damian.'

There were more voices. Girls too. He could hear them laughing. What had the first boy found? He sounded pretty worked up.

Maybe it was a squid. Squid sometimes got stranded on the shingle and once there had been a baby hammerhead, which was mistaken for a plesiosaur. It was half-rotten, so it hadn't looked like a shark at all and had to be taken away for identification. People were very disappointed when the papers revealed it wasn't a dinosaur, particularly Uncle Eugene. He went into such deep depression they had to adjust his medication.

'Damian! Come look at this!'

What were they yelling about? Oh no . . . maybe they'd found the rest of the rocket. It must have washed up nearby while he was inside the cave. Adam gritted his teeth and swore. What if they took it? He was planning to rebuild it. It was going to be his project for the summer holidays.

The voices were fainter now. He slid the piece of driftwood away slightly and spied on them through the crack. There they were, standing in a circle round a rock pool, staring and pointing. There were five of them . . . no, six. A younger girl had just arrived.

Two of the boys started arguing, one was shaking his head, the other nodding furiously. The fat one fetched a stick and poked around with it. He seemed nervous, then he turned his head away and pulled a face.

Adam couldn't see what they were looking at. He was at the wrong angle, there were too many people in the way. Perhaps it was a drowned dog or a dead body. Or part of a dead body? If so, which part? He shuddered and hoped it wasn't the head.

Suddenly, whatever it was started thrashing about. Everyone leapt back. The youngest girl shrieked, crouched down and hid her face in her skirt. Adam could see snapshots of convulsing limbs, but they were so blurred, there could have been any number of them. They could have been flesh or fins. Tentacles or tails.

Adam felt strangely detached, as if he was watching a film, utterly focused on the action framed by the crack in the cave. The rest of the world was cut off. It didn't exist.

Earlier, he'd thought of climbing the side of the cliff to get a better view, but he dismissed the idea. He wouldn't be welcome. He could sense he was witnessing something sinister. He decided to stay where he was.

Now the youngest girl was clinging to her sister and the tall boy with blond hair was looking around on the ground – searching for what? Ah, a pebble. No, not that one, too small. This one! He rubbed it on his trouser leg like a cricket ball and headed back to the pool and stopped at what he imagined was a safe distance.

Everyone else decided to look for pebbles too. Everyone copied the boy with blond hair. They took up their places around the rock pool again. The blond boy looked up at the cliffs, then without warning, he flicked his wrist back and threw his pebble down hard.

[15]

There was an ear-splitting shriek. The others had raised their arms, ready to throw their pebbles, but now the stones flew off target or were dropped as they scattered, screaming and shouting.

The thrashing in the rock pool had stopped, but they couldn't see that.

They were running away from the atrocity, wide-eyed and giggling, but not because it was funny – it was anything but funny. The youngest girl was pale and hysterical. She was half-tripping towards The Black Hole, panting and sobbing, trying to keep up with her sister.

'It's after me, Clare. Clare! . . . *Wai . . . t!*'

Adam drew back into the gloom of the cave. There was no time to put the driftwood in place. He held his breath as the boys thundered past.

'Jay! What if you killed it? What are we gonna . . .?'

'Shut your face . . . it was morphing! It's a morphing alien . . . *ruuuuuuuun!*'

Adam waited until they'd gone. The beach was deserted. Flicking his penknife open, he crept up to the rock pool to see what all the fuss was about.

*

It looked like a small, dead boy from where he was standing. Tragic as it was, nothing prepared him for his initial reaction to it, which was huge disappointment. He'd been expecting to find something else and while he was ashamed to admit it, he felt cheated, even annoyed.

It was only when he turned the damp, twisted body over with the fat boy's stick that he realized why the other kids had freaked out; its face wasn't entirely human. It was such a shock, he thought he was going to puke. He turned his head away and swallowed hard.

Having managed to control the contents of his stomach, he forced himself to look again. Instantly, he was overcome by

[16]

the Unknown Force that had spoken to him through the *ET* video when he was small. He could feel it sparkling in his veins like an electric charge. For a moment, he was paralysed. Then, the sensation stopped and with blinding clarity, he believed he'd been chosen to witness this vision, this miracle in the rock pool. And it *was* a miracle, finding an alien on his own patch. Even if it was dead. Here was all the proof he needed to show the cynics and the non-believers that he, Adam Lurie, had been right all along.

He knelt down and gazed at the corpse in awe.

The scalp, he noted, was covered in bluish-black bristles, almost as if it had been shaved. The skull was much smaller than his sister's, and out of proportion to the rest of its body which was roughly the size of a skinny five-year-old.

There was an injury to the left brow, which had puffed up and thrown the face out of symmetry. The slack grimace and the overcrowded, peg-like teeth that protruded from its lip-less mouth didn't comply with the human idea of beauty, but perhaps, where it had come from, it might have been considered handsome.

A fat bluebottle buzzed overhead and landed on the carcass. Adam batted it away in disgust, but it was persistent. It turned into a fight, with the bluebottle dodging under his arm and dive-bombing his ear. Finally, he pulled his trainer off, lobbed the fly onto the shingle and smothered it with sand. By now, he felt so protective towards his alien, he felt the slow, horrible death of the fly was justified.

He tried to imagine how his creature might have walked when it was alive. Its spine was curved, which might have been a deformity. There again, this particular species might have humps for sound biological reasons, like camels.

It looked nothing like any of the creatures in *Star Wars*. There were no tentacles, at least none that he could see. There were no extra limbs, no special breathing organs, none of the extraordinary features he would have expected to find on a life-form that had evolved in a radically different atmosphere.

On reflection, he wasn't all that surprised. It simply confirmed what he and Moses had suspected all along; there *were* habitable planets in other galaxies, similar to Earth. Therefore it wasn't in the least bit odd that this creature bore more than a passing resemblance to himself.

Pulling the neck of his T-shirt over his nose to mask the sweet, sickly smell, he leant over further to study its facial features more closely. The differences were subtle. It was like doing a 'Spot The Difference' puzzle – he knew there were differences in Picture 'A'(the alien's face) compared with Picture 'B' (his own) but he had to really concentrate hard to discover what they were.

Its eyes were closed. There were two of them, positioned on the front of the forehead, but the sockets were much shorter than his and sat in pouches of folded skin. There were no obvious cheekbones.

The nose was peculiar too. It was small with a sunken bridge but the main point of difference was this: there was no groove under it. No nose groove at all. The area below the nostrils was completely smooth.

To look at the rest of the body, which appeared to have two arms and two legs, he would have to remove the filthy rags it was wrapped in. Miracle or not, he was loath to do this with his bare hands in case the corpse was contaminated with deadly spores.

He almost went back to The Black Hole to fetch his goalie gloves when he remembered he had an empty crisp packet in his pocket – he'd been saving it for the book tokens on the back. He pulled it out, ate the last crumbs and decided that although it wasn't ideal, it was the nearest thing he had to a surgical glove.

Putting his hand inside the greasy bag, he uncurled the creature's fingers one by one and counted them. There were five, but the fourth and fifth fingers were almost half the size of the others. The fingernails on both little fingers were minuscule – no more than dots.

He studied the palms. Compared to his own, there were hardly any lines, just a single, deep crease. It was a Palm Reader's worst nightmare.

His grandmother, Marina, had read his palm once. She was a mystic and spent her life working the fairgrounds with Grandad Clem. When Adam was small, his mother used to dump him in Grandma's sweaty, red, skull-filled tent in his pushchair. Once, he'd chewed one of her tarot cards. She'd grabbed his hand, told him he had a particularly short life-line and predicted he'd come to a sticky end.

He wondered what fortune she could have foreseen in the floppy little hand he was holding. He shook it gently by the wrist. It was still slightly warm and pliable. No sign of rigor mortis. The poor thing must have died seconds before he arrived.

Adam felt ashamed to be human. Here lay the answer to the greatest mystery in the universe and it had been silenced for ever by a boy with a pebble. Why hadn't he tried to stop him? The kid hadn't been *that* big. He wasn't even as big as Sonny. He would never forgive himself. More to the point, nor would Moses. If Moses had been there, they could have done something.

He sighed and gave the thin wrist an apologetic squeeze. Suddenly, he felt a soft pulse beneath his fingers, which made him fling the hand away with a shriek. The hand sprang back. The alien sat up, flung both arms around him and fell back-wards into the rock pool with Adam pinned to his chest. He couldn't move.

They lay and screamed, eyeball to eyeball, until they both ran out of breath.

*

The tide was turning. Adam must have fainted in the alien's arms, which were draped loosely over his back. He pushed himself on to his knees. As he came to his senses, he realized with mounting panic that he had a monumental decision to make. If the alien had been dead, the right thing to do would be to take it to the authorities, who would let the whole world know about his extraordinary find.

He hadn't the faintest idea what to do now that the alien was resurrected.

His immediate thought was to hide it. He'd seen *ET* – he knew what could happen if extra-terrestrials fell into the wrong hands. They'd do experiments on him. It could kill him. He didn't want that on his conscience.

Nor did he want those kids coming back with their parents to look for it. That would steal his thunder.

The creature stared up at him with dull, green eyes. It looked very sick. He wasn't sure it would survive, but if it was going to die, he wanted it to die in peace. Then, and only then, he would contact NASA and allow them to perform an autopsy. He didn't like the idea, but he wasn't sentimental enough to let his personal feelings stand in the way of progress. He crouched down and scooped the creature up in his arms.

'Don't be scared. I'm not going to hurt you.'

It didn't struggle. Adam staggered clumsily back up the shingle. The creature lay awkwardly, but it wasn't heavy. It weighed less than Fay, a lot less. It wasn't so easy to slam-dunk her on to the sofa these days.

With a final look over his shoulder, he propped his alien against the cave entrance and crawled inside. Then he reached out, slid his hands under its arms and pulled it indoors where it collapsed in a soggy heap.

Adam lay down on the cave floor next to it. He put his knees up to his chin and rolled around to get rid of the stitch in his side. Having recovered, he decided the kindest thing to do was to lift the creature on to the lilo and let nature take its course.

If it died, at least it could die quietly on a soft bed where it wouldn't be attacked by dogs, pecked by birds or stoned by boys. He wondered whether to start the barbecue up to keep it warm, but what if it came from a cold planet, like Mars, where the temperature rarely went above freezing?

Maybe it was dying of heat exhaustion. He whipped the eiderdown back, but the alien grabbed it, pulled it over its head and turned to face the wall. Shy or cold? He couldn't tell.

Perhaps it was thirsty. Possibly it could survive on seawater, but everything he'd ever read told him that drinking seawater made people go mad. The same might apply to aliens. There was nothing to drink in the cave, only a can of Tango that Moses had left behind. If anything was likely to finish it off, that would.

He could fetch tap water, but could the alien tolerate the chemicals in it? Chlorine and fluoride might poison it. It might as well drink hemlock.

While he relished the idea of playing the saviour, he was only just beginning to realize what he was letting himself in for. The responsibility might be more of a burden than a pleasure. He wished he had a disciple to share it with, then, if it all went wrong, it wouldn't be all his fault.

'This is Captain Lurie to Starflight Commander Shoderu. Do you read me? Over.'

Radio silence.

By now, the creature had either gone into a coma or a deep sleep. The smell, which hadn't seemed so bad in the sea breeze was becoming really foul. Adam pushed the driftwood back a bit to let the air circulate. He lit more candles, put his goalie gloves on and went through the patient's clothing for clues.

He felt a small, square lump. He rooted among the folds and pulled out a brown bottle, possibly made of glass-like material with a cracked, black lid. There was a label on the front. It had got wet at some point, but there were still traces of scrawled writing done in an alien hand. The letters were similar to the ones on the rocket.

[21]

'Ohmigod – it's *his* rocket!'

Adam's eyes darted from the snuffling form of the sleeping alien to the metal tubes arranged on the floor.

'Ah! It's so obvious!'

He could have kicked himself for not putting two and two together earlier. Now everything was falling into place. The rocket was exactly the right size for its tiny pilot. It must have splashed down in the sea on a deliberate mission. Or something had gone wrong and it had crashed and broken up. The rest of the spacecraft burnt up on entry, which was why he hadn't found any more of it.

The alien had managed to crawl out of the pod, but had either half-drowned in the process and been washed up by the tide, or staggered out of the sea and collapsed in the rock pool, unseen until the gang of kids found him. Until, by divine intervention, Adam rescued him.

Was there a co-pilot? Adam hoped not. It was hard enough trying to nurse one extra-terrestrial. He wasn't sure he could manage two. He turned his attention back to the brown bottle and shook it gently. Something rattled inside. He unscrewed the lid at arm's length as if he was diffusing a bomb.

Nothing happened, so he looked inside. It was full of tablets. These must be the chemicals that allowed the creature to survive Earth's atmosphere. After all, drugs were used to expand the lungs of asthmatic humans to help them breathe. The school medical room was full of kids wheezing into their inhalers because they didn't want to do country dancing.

He would put the tablets to the test when the alien woke up. He'd offer it some and see how it reacted. He was tempted to drop one into its open mouth there and then, but maybe that wasn't how it was supposed to take its medication.

Maybe the tablets were supposed to go up its nose or somewhere even more private. Uncle Eugene said the French never swallowed pills, they always shoved them up their arse. If that was the case, he'd let it take its own tablets. Its backside could be anywhere and even with his goalie gloves on, he didn't like to look.

Adam put the bottle to one side and dug deeper into the pocket. There was nothing there, except a length of seaweed. It looked like bladderwrack, covered in warty bubbles that were asking to be popped.

He resisted – it might not be bladderwrack. It might be vegetation from one of Jupiter's moons: Europa, Ganymede, Io or even Callisto. The Voyager Space Probe had it on good evidence that there were oceans under the ice crust on Europa. Moses had told him and Uncle Eugene had confirmed it.

'Oh, that,' he'd said. 'They've known *that* since 1989.'

Adam did the responsible thing. He put the seaweed specimen into his crisp bag, rolled the top over, sealed it with a blob of chewing gum and put it in the supply cupboard. He might have to hand it over to NASA eventually for analysis, so he had to conduct himself as professionally as possible, given the circumstances.

He searched the alien's rags for more pockets. There was one on the other side and here, he found something of great interest – a piece of yellowish metal, a bit like the earth equivalent of a brass wing nut. It was stuck halfway down a rusty twist of metal, about four centimetres long. It might have been an ordinary screw, but Adam had his scientist's hat on and refused to jump to conclusions. One thought did spring to mind, however: it could be a fundamental part of the rocket.

The alien woke with a start. It sat up and narrowed its eyes, which almost disappeared into the folds of surrounding skin. Adam backed off, afraid that it might not be so friendly after all.

'Oh, I'm sorry. I was only looking. Here, you have it.'

He tossed the metal object into its lap. The creature fumbled with ill-equipped fingers and concentrated on loosening the wing nut, grumbling to itself.

'What is it?' Adam asked. 'Is it part of your spaceship?'

The alien ignored him, so he repeated the question louder.

'Is this part of your rocket?'

Still no response. It was ludicrous to assume the alien could understand English. He tried to communicate with sign language and with exaggerated arm movements gesticulated to the metal tubes arranged on the floor and made spaceship noises.

'See this? Is this your rocket?'

He picked up one of the fins and put it on the lilo.

'This . . . is it yours?'

Adam nodded his head, as if to encourage an answer.

'This is from your spaceship . . . yes?'

The alien looked at him quizzically, then nodded too. It stretched its fingers shakily and touched the fin.

'I knew it!' Adam whispered under his breath. 'I knew it!'

He shook the creature warmly by the hand.

'Welcome to Planet Earth. I am Adam Lurie.'

He pointed to himself, in case there was a misunderstanding.

'Me . . . Adam! I am A-dam. Do you understand?'

The alien nodded, slapped its chest and replied, 'Squeep . . . Sqippi.'

It was hard to make out what it was trying to say, its mouth was so crammed full of teeth, but it sounded a bit like 'Skippy' to Adam.

'Do you mind if I call you Skippy?'

The alien shook its head.

'Skippy it is, then!'

Now it was rocking backwards and forwards excitedly.

''S *'ave* it,' it insisted. ''S *'ave* it!'

It sounded like, 'Let's have it.' What was it after? Ah, it wanted the rocket fin! Adam put it on the lilo.

'Of *course* you can have it.'

Skippy was delighted and became obsessed with trying to insert his rusty screw into one of its holes. Clearly, he was trying to fix it.

'I'll help you later, when you're feeling stronger.' Adam told him. 'By the way, shouldn't you take one of these?'

[24]

He shook some of the tablets into his hand. Dutifully, Skippy opened his mouth. Adam didn't know how many to give him. 'Say no to drugs', they said at school. Mind you, Sonny never said no. And he smoked.

'How many. One . . . Two?' He held his fingers up.

'Nje . . . Dy,' said Skippy.

At first, Adam thought he'd said 'Jedi.' But then he realized that was ridiculous and decided Skippy was asking him a question: 'I . . . die?'

'You're not going to die,' he reassured him.' I'll look after you.'

Skippy swallowed two pills, then settled down and fiddled endlessly with his wing nut and fin. Left to his own devices, he might have carried on like that all afternoon.

Adam wasn't sure what to do with himself. Here he was, a ten-year-old boy in charge of an alien. If it ever got out, he'd be in all the papers. He would be world famous. Everyone would know the name of Adam Lurie. He might even be a question in a history exam.

Question Number One: Who was the first person to discover Intelligent Life from another planet?
Answer: Adam Lurie!

He'd probably be Sir Adam Lurie by then. He was bound to get a knighthood. That would stick it right up Sonny. They'd all have to respect him – Mum, Dad. Fay. Even Uncle Eugene couldn't fail to be impressed by this little coup.

It was so tempting to run home and tell them all but something stonger told him not to tell a living soul. Skippy hadn't come here to be paraded like a freak for his own gain. But it was so tempting . . .

His daydream was interrupted by voices drifting through the gap he'd created in the doorway. The hairs stood up on the back of his neck. He tiptoed over to the driftwood, finger to his lips, begging Skippy to stay silent. It was that boy, Damian, with his father.

'It was over there, Dad! It was going nuts. Thrashing about and that.'

They were heading for the rock pool. There was nothing there, of course. They'd be gone soon – the father not believing his own son about the alien, the son not believing his own father could call him a liar.

Adam put the driftwood back in place. What he needed now was a plan of action. If he'd known an alien was going to arrive, he would have prepared earlier. He had no idea what he was going to do in the long term, but right now, he had to fetch some emergency supplies – food, clothing and bottled water. It wasn't going to be easy with Fay hanging around. He hoped she was sitting on a slow pony in a field far away, followed by a sleep-over at her best friend, Paris William's house.

No one must know about Skippy.

Chapter Three

Unfortunately, Fay hadn't gone pony riding or round to Paris's or under the wheels of a bus. She was sitting on a bench in the workshop at the back of Lurie's Motors, playing with a Beanie Baby donkey.

'Trot on, Twonk! Sonny, *watch*! Twonk's trotting!'

She spotted Adam hovering in the doorway.

'Oh, there you are. What have you been doing?'

'Playing aliens.'

He couldn't resist it. No one was likely to believe him, were they? Fay pulled a face.

'Yeah, right. I'm not stupid. What have you really been doing?'

Sonny was in there with his mates, Slash and Ghetto, having a garage-fest. They were doing up their motorbikes ready for the Stevenage Run the following Saturday. They were supposed to be going to the open-air concert at Knebworth, but what they were really going for was a fight.

Rumour had it that a rival bike gang called The Impalers were riding up from Alexandra Palace on the same day. Slash's girlfriend, Cornelia Schatz, had copped off with their president, Vic the Inhaler, at a funfair in Margate. She was last seen sitting on the sissy bar of his Kawasaki with two coconuts stuffed down her jumper.

Slash hadn't even liked Cornelia much, but somehow, Sonny managed to convince him that stealing another member's old lady was a hanging offence and if he let Vic get away with it, everyone would think he was chicken.

Slash didn't want to be a chicken, so he agreed to seek

revenge. This meant that Sonny, Ghetto and the handful of other losers that rode with The Outcasts were obliged by law to give him a helping hand.

'One on all, all on one!'

They were going to 'ratpack' Vic. They were going to ambush him, duff him up and rip the sacred patch off his jacket. They'd talked about nothing else for weeks.

Adam thought it was pathetic. Sonny's Outcasts weren't proper Hell's Angels – not like his dad's old chapter, The Hung Priests. They were scary men, the stuff of nightmares. Adam had seen photos. Chas had the best ones turned into posters which were stuck all round the walls of his motorbike shop.

They all had weird names: Axel the Greece, Mouldy Martin, Barf Bartholomew. None of them weighed less than twenty stone, and they all wore leathers, long beards and threatening scowls. Most of them were either inside or dead now. The ones who hadn't overdosed had died on their bikes.

When Chas was reliving his past, which he often did after a few cans, he would repeat his favourite 'Hell's Angels' Funerals I Have Been To' stories. These consisted of a solemn procession of bikers following the hearse of The Fallen, who would be forever remembered by the length of the skid mark he left behind – twenty-five metres in the case of Mad Mac Fitzacherly, who had a head-on collision with a lorry full of frozen cod.

Tales like these had been Sonny's bedtime stories and he thrived on them. When he grew up, he was going to go one better than his dad – Chas had always followed the pack; Sonny was going to lead.

As soon as he'd got his licence, he organized his own motorbike gang with its own code and customs. He instructed Ghetto to design a logo to go on the back of their leather jackets. This was taken to a trophy shop and turned into patches, which had the name of their gang embroidered on the bottom rocker – The Outcasts. Sonny appointed himself President.

At first, there was just the three of them, but as there was nothing exciting for a young hooligan to do on a rainy day by the north coast, membership grew rapidly. The sale of bomber jackets boomed. Lurie's Motors did a roaring trade. Old ladies hid indoors.

Adam remained unimpressed.

OK, all the girls fancied Sonny because he had the best bike and looked fit but he couldn't grow a beard to save his life. Ghetto worked for Pizza Hut and his mum wouldn't let him ride anything bigger than a Vespa and although Slash was huge and rode like a maniac, he was just a big softy really. He'd cried his eyes out when his hamster died.

Adam stopped hovering at the workshop doorway and went in. He was on safe ground. Sonny wouldn't dare shoot him in front of Slash and Ghetto. They'd tell his mum.

'Hi, Slash. All right, Ghetto?'

'Yo, Adam! How's it going?'

Ghetto had babysat for Adam once. It had been a riot. They'd had some of Chas's lager, played darts and watched *The Great Escape* on video. Towards the end of the evening, Ghetto had dropped his leathers, bent over and shown Adam his Death's Head tattoo. Slash had drawn it for him with a compass and ink.

'I would have done it myself,' Ghetto explained. 'But I couldn't reach.'

Adam wanted one just like it, only not on his buttock, so Ghetto drew one on his belly and coloured it in with black and red biros. It looked the business. Ghetto had been to art school, and it showed. Adam's mother hadn't been quite so impressed. He had to have a medical the next day and the school nurse got a nasty shock when she lifted his vest.

The Death's Head refused to die. They tried everything to get it off – soap, washing-up liquid. Even lighter fuel. Uncle Eugene said he had some acid that would do the job and was most offended when no one took him up on the suggestion. In the end his mother covered it up with elastoplast on school days and attacked it now and again with a rough flannel.

Adam went and stood by Sonny, who ignored him. He was busy spraying Baby's gas tank with Flame Orange paint. Even Adam had to admit she was looking good. The front and back fenders had been chopped, the windshield had gone and the big, comfortable seat had been replaced with a neat, uncomfortable one.

Baby used to have regular handlebars, but Chas had made a pair of high bars out of some metal chair legs so Sonny could ride her with his arms above his head, like an ape. Adam put his head on one side and examined Sonny's paint job.

'You've missed a bit . . . where's Mum?'

'College.'

She was doing an accountancy course. She was going to get a degree and work in the city. Last year, she was going to be an aromatherapist. Anything to get away from motorbikes and motherhood.

'Where's Dad?'

'Casualty.'

'With Uncle Eugene?'

Sonny nodded. It was nothing new. Uncle Eugene had built a laboratory in his bedsit and filled it with all manner of exciting chemicals, some of which were highly explosive. So far, he'd had plastic surgery to his groin, a detached retina and a perforated eardrum.

'You owe me one, 'Sonny scowled.' Karen forced me to clean out the python and I *think* we know who's turn it was, don't we?'

Sonny always called his parents by their christian names – Chas and Karen. He had 'Chas and Kaz' tattooed on his bicep. Grandad Clem had done it for him as a fifteenth birthday present. It had gone septic.

'I owe you nothing,' said Adam.

Sonny pretended to rip off his own testicles as if to remind him about the incident with the heavy book.

'I think you do. I want you to look after Fay till Chas gets back. Karen said you've got to help her practise her violin.'

'No, she didn't. You're lying.'

Fay swung her feet against the workbench. 'I don't want to practise my violin!'

'Yeah, you do,' said Sonny. 'Bye-bye.'

Fay screwed up her face and started to cry. 'Oh . . . how come I'*m* the only one who has to play the stupid violin? It's not fair!'

Sonny played his trump card. 'I'll tell Mum.'

'Ooooooooooh!' sang Slash and Ghetto.

Fay ran out of the workshop and Sonny steered Adam forcibly out into the yard.

'Off you go, Dweeb.'

Adam climbed the back stairs up to the flat, seething. How was he supposed to get supplies for Skippy with Fay hanging around? She'd want to know what he was doing, why he was doing it and where he was going. She'd rumble him.

Fay was in her bedroom, sobbing theatrically. He ignored her, found a plastic carrier bag and started to look through all the cupboards for suitable alien food. Given that he hadn't a clue what Skippy's natural diet was, he was going to have to take pot luck. Jelly cubes? Variety pack of cereal? Gravy granules?

'What 'you doing? What's that for?'

It was Fay.

'Mind your own business. Practise your violin.'

'Why should I? Why are you putting gravy in that bag? What are you doing with Mum's fizzy water? Where are you going?'

Her violin was on the kitchen table. He picked it up, rammed it under her chin and parked her in front of the music stand. She stuck out her lower lip.

'Hate you!'

'Hate you more.'

Adam sidled past her, went to his room and shut the door.

[31]

He was looking for his radio torch. Skippy might know a way of using the radio waves to contact his planet. The beam on this torch was more powerful than the one he kept in the cave. They could use it to signal to approaching spacecraft. Skippy's commander was bound to send out a search party at some point.

Adam was looking through his wardrobe to find a suitable change of clothing, but everything was far too big for Skippy. He stood on a chair and opened the top cupboard. There was some stuff he'd grown out of in it – dressing-up clothes he'd had when he was little.

There was a fireman's helmet, a ridiculous reindeer costume left over from the nursery school Christmas play and a pair of red, cotton mechanics overalls with a spanner embroidered on the pocket. They looked about the right size.

'Do you want to play dressing up?'

The midget violinist had come back to haunt him.

'Go away, Fay.'

'Oh, plea . . . se! I'll be the beautiful princess and you can be the mechanic and mend my golden carriage.'

Adam stuck two fingers up and squeezed past. He went to the bathroom and locked the door.

'Let me in, Adam!'

'No.'

There was a green, sponge frog filled with cheap soap in the cabinet. Paris had given it to Fay for her birthday but the soap had brought her out in a rash. He threw it in the bag along with a hand towel and the remains of the toilet roll. Suddenly, something whacked him sharply round the ankles.

'Ow! What the . . . ?'

Fay had pushed her violin bow through the gap under the locked door and was thrashing it about wildly. Adam stood on it.

'Adam, get off. Let me in. I need the toilet!'

'No, you don't.'

He pulled the bow into the bathroom. She was beating the door with her fists now.

'Quick! I'm desperate! Open the door or I'll tell!'

'Wait.'

He undid the lock. He'd fixed Sonny's toothbrush into the bow, like an arrow. The second she burst in, he pulled it back and fired it at her head. She retaliated by pushing him into the bath.

'Stupid little girl,' he muttered.

She stuck her tongue out, '*Ner!*'

He ran off, slamming the door on her.

Adam went into the front room. The book that Uncle Eugene had lent him was lying under a pile of newspaper splattered with soft, smelly python droppings. It was too big to go in the plastic bag, so he tucked it under his arm.

A little voice wailed from the bathroom, 'There's no toi . . . let paper!'

He smiled and let himself out of the front door.

*

As Adam raced down to The Black Hole with his stash, he hoped with every atom in his body that Skippy was still in the cave.

Anything could have happened. He could have died by now. He could have wandered off and got lost. Or he could have been rescued by his own kind. They might have been watching from behind a cloud all along, or through the periscope of an interstellar-solar submarine.

Nothing seemed impossible any more. In Uncle Eugene's book, there was a page all about 'The Principle of Plenitude'. It was a complicated law of physics, but what it boiled down to was this: anything that can happen, *will* happen. And it all seemed to be happening today.

The book, which had been written by a highly respected astrophysicist, had also suggested that since Earth had produced the right conditions for life to appear, we should *expect* life to be widespread throughout the galaxy. What Adam *hadn't* expected was for it to appear quite so close to home.

There was no sign of Skippy on the beach. Adam put his bag and book down and peered into the cave entrance. He'd blown out most of the candles before he left, so it was hard to see anything. He took his radio torch out of the bag and turned it on.

'Skippy?'

There was no answer.

'Skip? It's me! Please don't be dead.'

Adam flashed the torch across the lilo. There he was, still rocking backwards and forwards, examining the wing nut with infinite patience. Adam climbed through the hole and went over to him.

'Still not got it working then? Want me to have a go with my spanner?'

Skippy didn't acknowledge him at all. It was as if he was invisible. Adam sat down next to him and held up the plastic carrier bag.

'Look, I've brought some food. I thought you might be hungry.'

Skippy showed no interest in the bag. Instead, he flung his arms round Adam's neck and held him tight. The hug didn't stop. It made Adam feel distinctly uncomfortable.

It was nice that Skippy was so pleased to see him, but the hug was too intimate for his liking. He wouldn't dream of cuddling Moses like that. Moses would have decked him for sure.

'Captain Lurie to Starflight Commander Shoderu. The native is friendly. A bit too friendly. Do you think it might be gay? Over.'

'*This is Commander Shoderu. Only one way to find out, Captain. Ask if it knows the way to Uranus.*'

Adam had nothing against gay aliens, he just hated the

thought of physical contact with anybody. He didn't even like it when his mother kissed him any more. He couldn't bear to see people touching each other, even on TV.

It had all started last Easter when, riddled with jealousy, he'd sneaked into Sonny's bedroom to steal some of his chocolate egg. Sonny had told everyone he was going to the cinema, so Adam had been very surprised to find him lying face down on the carpet, groaning.

At first, he thought he'd fallen over and was struggling to get up, but then he realized he was lying on top of his girl-friend. Sonny hadn't noticed him, so he'd stood and watched for a minute to make sure he wasn't imagining things.

It wasn't a pretty sight. Traumatized, as if he'd witnessed a road accident, Adam backed silently out of the room. The only person he'd confessed to was his uncle. On hindsight, it had been a mistake. Uncle Eugene had been eating his break-fast at the time and was so revolted he snorted a lump of scrambled egg out of his nose.

'I don't want to *know*!' he shuddered. 'Stop it, You're turn-ing my stomach. Quick, talk about Einstein's Theory of Relativity! Particle physics! I can't eat my bacon now.'

Uncle Eugene hated physical contact too. He'd never had a girlfriend, or a boyfriend for that matter. On the numerous occasions he'd been carted off to hospital, the nurses had to pin him down before he'd let a doctor anywhere near him. He'd scream at them:

'Get off me, you harpies!'

The strange thing was, he was able to show a great deal of affection towards Helium, his stinky old labrador. Helium was allowed to slobber all over him. In fact, he was positively encouraged.

'I can relate to dogs,' Uncle Eugene insisted.

Skippy continued to hold Adam in an affectionate neck-lock. Adam tried to convince himself that this was how Skippy related to his folk back home. Maybe the neck-hug was their traditional greeting. After all, look what footballers got up to on this planet. Kissing each other and what-not. Eeeuch! That's why he hated playing.

By now, Adam had a crick in his neck, so he gave Skippy a self-conscious squeeze and tried to interest him in the jelly he'd brought.

Skippy didn't get on too well with the jelly. Adam tore off one of the rubbery little squares and offered it to him, but he didn't know what to do with it.

'Eat it, Skippy, it's nice. It's raspberry.'

He held it out on the flat of his hand. Skippy picked it up between his finger and thumb but he was distressed by its stickiness and tried to shake it off as if it was a bloodsucking bug.

He was equally unimpressed with the cereal. Adam had never expected him to go for the All-Bran, no one liked that, so he'd opened *his* favourite, which was chocolate flavoured.

Skippy put a handful in his mouth. A few seconds later, his eyes began to bulge. Adam slapped him hard on the back, but he couldn't shift the blockage. How was it going to look to NASA if he choked their first genuine alien to death on a Coco Pop?

Adam tried to think back to when his mother had done her first-aid course. She used to practise on him, putting him in the recovery position and bandaging all his limbs until he looked like an Egyptian mummy. Uncle Eugene came round in the middle of a session once and thought he must have fallen off the roof.

What were you supposed to do if someone had something stuck in their throat? It all came flooding back to him.

'Open the patient's mouth and try to remove the blockage.'

He tried, but Skippy bit him.

'If the patient is a child, put him over your knee and thump the small of his back. If this fails, try tipping him upside down and let gravity do its work.'

It wasn't easy tipping Skippy upside down. He was too long and he didn't like it one bit.

[36]

'Skippy, hold still! I'm trying to save your life!'

In the struggle, Adam accidentally elbowed him in the stomach. The Coco Pop shot out and twanged off the side of the cave. All was well.

Skippy liked the mineral water. He drank the lot, then sat back down, burped and continued to play with his wing nut. Adam felt put out. While he understood the importance of the wing nut, he thought Skippy might have been a bit more interested in his new environment and the food Adam had brought at great personal risk.

Skippy wasn't in the least bit grateful to him for rescuing the crate of rocket parts either. He seemed in no hurry to look at them at all. Still, Adam excused him. He was probably suffering from rocket-lag. It was an honour he was here at all. Saviours weren't supposed to sulk.

He dug around in the bag for the radio torch and switched it on. It crackled in between stations. He thrust it under Skippy's nose.

'It's a radio. Ra-di-o. I thought you could contact someone with it?'

Skippy looked confused. 'Squip!' he said, nodding his head.

'Yes . . . it's for you.'

Adam closed Skippy's elongated fingers around it. Skippy refused to speak, but there was another voice:

'Who are you talking to?'

Adam whisked round angrily. He'd forgotten to put the driftwood back in place. Fay was peering at him through the hole!

'How did you know I was here?'

She'd brought her violin with her. And Twonk.

'I followed you. Who are you talking to?'

She craned her neck to try and see past him. He sprang off the bed and dodged about with his arms outspread to block her view.

'No one . . . go away!'

[37]

'No, I'm coming in and you can't stop me.'

Adam leapt across the cave, dragged the driftwood over the entrance and trapped her knee.

'Fay, get your leg out or I'll squash you. I mean it.'

'No.'

He screwed his face up and started to apply pressure.

'Ouch! If you don't let me in, I'll tell Sonny!'

Adam knew she would, so he snatched Twonk. Checkmate.

'All right,' he said, 'but if you breathe a word to Mum or Dad or Sonny, I'll pull Twonk's head off.' Fay's face fell.

'Adam, you wouldn't!'

'I would.'

He had the little donkey by the tail and throat and started to pull.

'OK, OK, I promise! *Please* don't hurt him.'

Fay reached out to rescue Twonk, but Adam was too quick and shoved him in his pocket.

'No, I'm keeping hold of him, in case you break your promise,' he said. 'Deal?'

She nodded tearfully. He let her into the cave, blocked the entrance and reluctantly, made the introductions.

'Fay, this is Skippy – Skippy, I'm afraid this is my sister.'

To Adam's disappointment, Fay didn't scream in terror. She just looked at him quizzically and whispered behind her hand, 'He looks weird.'

Adam tutted, 'Of course he looks weird, he's from another planet, stupid.'

'Really . . .? Really, *really*? Which one?'

'He didn't say.'

Fay opened her eyes wide. 'Does he speak?'

Adam nodded.

'A little bit. He told me his name anyway.'

Fay waved at Skippy shyly.

'Hello!'

Skippy waved back. He mumbled something, which sounded like 'Tungatatta'.

Fay laughed.

'Tungytatta? That must be his word for hello! Tungytatta Skippy!'

She sat next to him on the lilo, wafting her nose at the smell.

'Pwhoar. He's a bit stinky!' She prodded his chest. 'You're stinky. I expect you've had a long journey.'

'Do you have to be so rude?' Adam said. 'He's been through hell. Look, I really don't want you here and nor does he.'

Skippy put his arm round her.

'See, Addy? He likes me!'

'So? He likes me too.'

Adam felt jealous. His sister was chattering away to his alien just like she did to Paris Williams, only in a mumsy, high-pitched voice. She was turning the most important revelation since the coming of Christ into a game of Mummies and Daddies.

'Is that your rocket? It's very nice. Do you want to listen to some music?'

She turned the radio on. It was playing an old David Bowie song. Fay knew it. Her mum played it in the car. She started to sing along.

'This is Major Tom to Ground Control. I'm stepping on the moo . . . oon. And I'm floating in a most peculiar way . . .'

She broke in, 'Do you come from the moon, Skippy?'

Adam rolled his eyes.

'Of course he doesn't come from the moon, stupid! The moon is uninhabitable. There's no water there for a start, no food.'

'How do you know? You've never been.' Fay tossed her blonde ponytail. 'In any case, maybe that's why he's come to Earth, because there's no food on the moon. He's very thin.'

'I tried to feed him but he didn't like anything I gave him.' Adam confessed. 'Although he nearly ate some cereal.'

Fay thought carefully.

'I think it's because of his teeth,' she said. 'They're all piggeldy. He can probably only manage soft things, like a baby. Is he a baby?'

'No, of course he's not a baby.'

'How do you know?'

Adam clenched his fists in exasperation.

'If he was a baby he wouldn't be able to fly a rocket, would he? Anyway Mrs Know-it all, I gave him soft food and he still didn't like it, *OK*?'

He thrust the jelly packet in her face. Fay shrugged.

'Maybe he doesn't like raspberry. Anyway, sugar is bad for your teeth. He needs something with lots of goodness in.'

She was just parroting Mum, but, in a funny way, Adam found it comforting. She sounded as if she knew what she was doing even if she didn't.

'Winkles!' she announced. 'Go to the seafood stall and get him a pint of winkles. I bet he'd like those.'

'You don't think he'd choke?'

'No. They're very slimy, aren't they? I'll look after him until you get back.'

Adam looked at her in disbelief.

'No way am I leaving him with you, Fay.'

It wasn't that he didn't trust her exactly, he just didn't want to share him. He sat down and folded his arms. Fay was stroking Skippy's bristly head.

'You stay here and I'll go, then.'

Mr Perry's seafood stall was in the high street about twenty minutes walk away. There was a main road. If Fay got run over, it would be his fault for sending her. Everyone would blame him. He wasn't having that.

'You're not allowed to cross the road on your own.'

'I'll be all right.'

Adam shook his head.

'Na. You're rubbish at it. You don't look properly.'

'So come with me.'

But he didn't want to leave Skippy on his own. On the

other hand, he didn't want him to starve.

It would be all his fault for not fetching winkles. Everyone would blame him . . .

'Oh, all right. I'll go. Just don't do anything silly and don't leave Skippy on his own.'

Skippy was dozing off anyway. He couldn't come to much harm, surely. Fay waved him off impatiently.

'Go on, then.'

He left. He ran all the way there, bought a pint of winkles and ran all the way back again. The sight that greeted him made his heart sink.

Skippy was standing in the sea, stark naked. Fay was washing him all over with her sponge frog. Adam marched across the shingle and jabbed her in the back.

'Fay!'

She span round. 'What?' She put her hands on her hips defiantly. '*What*? He was dirty, so I'm just giving him a wash. He doesn't mind, do you, Skippy?'

Skippy stood there, unprotesting, his body leaning awkwardly, goose pimples all over his flesh. Adam snatched the sponge off her.

'Cover him up! He can't go round like that.'

Skippy's teeth were chattering.

'Fancy an alien having a little thingy like yours,' said Fay.

Adam grabbed her sleeve.

'Shut *up*! You shouldn't even be *looking*! If he freezes to death, it'll be your fault. Put the towel round him!'

Fay wasn't sure what she'd done wrong, but she did as she was told and wrapped the towel round Skippy's shoulders. It only came down to his chest. Adam shouted at her.

'Not like that! Round his waist!'

'You stole my froggy sponge,' she pouted. 'I'm telling!'

Skippy followed her back to the cave like a lamb.

Adam was having problems trying to stuff Skippy's limbs in the mechanic's outfit. In the end, he admitted defeat and had to ask Fay for help.

'Only if you say sorry for shouting at me for washing him.'

'Why should I?'

Eventually, the sight of Skippy half-in and half-out of his clothing was more than he could stomach and he found himself apologizing against his will.

'Oh, all right. *Sorry*. There. I've said it.'

Fay smiled and having practised on hundreds of oddly shaped dolls with stiff, unyielding limbs, she had Skippy dressed in no time. The overalls were a bad fit across his back because of his curved spine and the legs were too short. She wasn't happy with the result.

'He looks silly like that, Adam. Couldn't you find anything more stylish?'

'No. You kept interrupting me, remember?'

Fay lowered her head.

'I'm sorry. I didn't know.'

She really *was* sorry. Adam could see that. He wished he could find it in himself to be kinder to her. He didn't hate Fay, it was just that everyone else seemed to like her so much. Sonny thought she was cute. Dad called her his princess. Mum spent loads of money on her. Yet she wouldn't buy him that telescope.

Being horrid to Fay was a habit he couldn't break. If he was nice to her, he was afraid he'd look weak. Anyway, why would he want to hang around with his little sister? They had nothing in common, no great secret to share. At least, not until now.

Skippy enjoyed the winkles. After he'd eaten, he sat down on the lilo, yawned and rocked backwards and forwards as he always did. Adam picked up Fay's violin.

'Play it for him.'

She wrinkled her nose up.

'I hate playing that violin. How come Mum makes me learn the violin and not you?'

'She loves you more.'

Fay looked surprised.

'She doesn't.'

'Yeah, she does.'

He put the violin in her lap.

'Go on, play it for Skippy. Please, Fay? We've got to go back soon and I need him to be asleep when I tie him up.'

Adam slid the leather belt out of his jeans.

'Don't look at me like that. I've got to do this or he might escape.'

Fay picked up her violin bow and started to play.

Chapter Four

Adam still had the beanie donkey in his pocket, but Fay hadn't given him any reason to pull its head off. In fact, over the next few days, she had never been less irritating.

It had got to the point where, instead of *pretending* to like her because he needed her help, there had been moments recently when he genuinely thought she was quite nice.

Like the time he took the last pint of milk for Skippy and Fay covered up for him. The time she sold her favourite doll, 'Diddles' to Paris Williams so she could buy church candles – big, thick ones that would burn all night, so Skippy didn't have to sleep in the dark.

Then there was the time Skippy was sick. It was just like human vomit and it made Adam heave, but Fay cleared it up without being asked, without any fuss. She worried constantly about his health.

'If Skippy gets ill, I mean really ill, we'll have to take him to a doctor, Adam.'

He told her that was impossible. They couldn't make an appointment without Mum, and anyway, what would a human doctor know about alien medicine?

'But what if he dies?'

Did she really think he hadn't thought about that? Keeping an alien alive and well was exhausting. Adam hadn't slept properly for days. He spent every waking moment on Skippy duty, thinking up excuses for why he had to leave the house so early every day – explaining why he'd put his breakfast bacon in his pocket – trying to find safe times to empty his mother's mineral water into his sports flask and replace the original stuff with tap water.

With the best will in the world, he knew he couldn't keep it up for ever. Skippy's greatest chance of survival was on his own planet. Adam would have to mend the rocket and send him home. The right thing to do – the *kind* thing to do was to let him go. And he could be kind. He would be kinder than Fay. He would be saintly!

'Skippy won't die,' he told her. 'He'll be fine. Trust me.'

Shortly after, he found her standing on the toilet seat so she could reach the medicine cabinet. She had removed the plastic instruments from her toy nurse's kit and was filling it with proper equipment – bandages, cough medicine, a thermometer.

Adam wished he'd thought of it and was jealous, but while he accused Fay of making a fuss, he felt a pang of fondness for her which he couldn't seem to get rid of. He did his utmost to disguise it, especially in public, but occasionally he slipped up and was pleasant to her.

People were starting to notice. Why, his mother asked, were the two of them no longer kicking each other's shins under the table? Why had Adam given Fay his slice of lemon tart? Why was Adam happy to take his sister down to the beach without being asked? Was he ill?

Sonny caught them with their heads together in Adam's bedroom. This was unheard of. He became suspicious and accused them of plotting against him.

'No we're not, we're arguing!' Adam lied. 'Aren't we, Fay?'

'Yeah, stupid ugly boy,' she agreed, jabbing him in the eye.

He twisted her nose, she screamed. Sonny rushed to her defence.

'Stop picking on her, Dweeb, or I'll do you!'

'Oh yeah?'

Sonny pinned Adam to the floor, sat on his chest and twisted his nose violently, as if he was tuning in a radio.

'Yeah! Karen's going on a retreat to Yorkshire tomorrow and then there'll be no one to hear . . . you . . . scream. Now, leave her alone!'

Adam rolled over with his face in his hands but as soon as Sonny was out of the room, he sat up and grinned. Fay looked relieved. She was getting confused with all the double-bluffing.

'We weren't really arguing, were we, Adam?' she whispered.

'No. We were thinking what to give Skippy for his tea today.'

He didn't dare tell her about sending him home yet. He needed her to stay happy and willing for a while. She'd done everything he'd asked so far. It would be easy enough to persuade her to steal the parts he needed from the workshop. His dad wouldn't miss them and no one would ever suspect sweet little Fay.

He'd been thinking about how to fix the rocket all night. Surrounded by various books, *A Guide To Interstellar Flight*, *Everyman's Book of Rockets* and several motorcycle manuals, he'd stayed up until three in the morning drawing a scale model based on all the tubes he'd found. It included a very detailed view of the rotor.

He'd indicated roughly where he thought the engine should go, where the pilot would sit and how the controls might work. It looked quite convincing on paper, but although he was very clued-up about engines and understood the basic theory of space flight, there were considerable gaps in his knowledge – he couldn't suss the whole thing out single-handed.

He was going to have to hoodwink Uncle Eugene into supplying the answers and possibly the chemicals.

He'd decided to invite himself round, and armed with his drawing, pretend that his school project for the holidays was to design and build a working model rocket. Once he'd explained there would be extra points for the pupil who managed to launch it the highest, Uncle Eugene wouldn't be able to resist going into teacher-mode and show him how it ought to be done. Adam chuckled out loud.

'What's so funny?' asked Fay.

'Nothing,' he said. 'You wouldn't mind borrowing some

parts from Dad's workshop when he's not looking, would you? It's to help Skippy.'

If it was to help Skippy, she would have agreed to murder the Pope.

'OK. But can we go and see him now? Only his wrists will get sore if we keep him tied up too long and he'll be hungry.'

Adam nodded.

'Soon as Mum's gone. We'll go down to The Black Hole and try him with pizza.'

It was what was left over from last night. Fay tapped her Barbie bag.

'Good idea. And I'm bringing my picture dictionary so I can teach him some words. The book's a bit babyish but I haven't got anything else. Is that OK?'

'Yeah, fine. Whatever.'

She accepted this begrudging crumb of praise and beamed with pride. Their mother came into the kitchen with her suitcase.

'Going on a picnic? I'm so pleased to see you two getting along. Why *are* you?'

'We're not. I'm only doing it because she's paying me,' said Adam.

He flashed his eyes at Fay to back him up, so she counted out the money on her fingers.

'I give him twenty pence if he lets me play with him and . . . um . . . ten pence if he lets me watch one of his videos and . . . how much do I have to pay to come in your room, Adam?'

'Fifty pence,' he lied.

His mother shook her head.

'Adam Lurie, you're heartless.'

He shrugged.

'How much will you give me to look after her while you're away?'

'Nothing! You should do it out of brotherly love.'

Adam turned on his heel.

'Love? *Ugh*! No money, no picnic for the brat.'

[47]

Fay put her head in her hands and pretended to bawl. His mother got her purse out.

'All right then . . . a pound.'

'A *pound*? Mum, you're going for a whole *week*! Two pounds fifty and that's my final offer.'

He folded his arms. The minicab driver rang the doorbell. She fiddled in her purse and slapped some coins on the table.

'You,' she said, 'are turning me into a really bad mother.'

'Thanks, Mum. Bye!'

She bent down to kiss Fay.

'That's not real crying, Fay. Be a good girl for Adam. If he does anything horrid to you, tell Dad and don't give him any more money. Bye!'

She struggled out with her bags. Adam pocketed the money.

'Is it enough for three ice-creams?' Fay asked. 'I bet Skippy would like ice-cream.'

'He might prefer beer,' said Adam. 'You've got to stop treating him like a kid. He's an intelligent adult. He's an astronaut, not one of your soppy mates.'

*

When they got to The Black Hole, Adam unstrapped Skippy and told Fay to stay with him until he came back. It was a risk he had to take. Fay couldn't believe her luck.

'Oh! OK. Where are you going?'

'Uncle Eugene's.'

Fay took the pizza out of her bag and handed Skippy a slice. She waved Adam off, thrilled to have Skippy all to herself. She loved him because all he wanted to do was love her back. She could make him do anything, pretty much. He trusted her completely. She chattered softly as he ate.

'I don't think you're as old as Adam thinks. He doesn't know everything. For all he knows, you could be a little boy alien who's lost his daddy. Maybe he drowned in the sea. Oh, I'm sorry if he did, Skippy.'

[48]

The belt had left red marks on his wrists. Fay rubbed them gently with her thumb. Skippy seemed very quiet this morning, so after he'd eaten the pizza she gave him two of his tablets with some mineral water, which perked him up.

She noticed his trousers were wet again, which was hardly surprising since he'd been tied up all night. He didn't seem bothered about it. Even so, she gave him some clean clothes and put a bucket out for him. She would persuade Adam to strap him down just by one hand in future.

Skippy was pacing around the cave in his underwear, right up on his toes. He seemed agitated and was chuntering to himself.

'I can't understand a word you're saying!' sighed Fay. 'Come over here, little spaceman.'

She took the picture dictionary out of her bag and patted the bed. He sat down, put his head on her shoulder and stroked her hair.

'*Bukur,*' he said. '*Bukur.*'

Fay patted his hand.

'That's right, Skippy, it's a book!'

She had great plans for him this morning. She fancied herself as a teacher and was determined to find out what Skippy was capable of.

*

Uncle Eugene had a crashing hangover when Adam arrived. He answered the door in his pyjamas. It clearly wasn't a good time to call, so Adam made an excuse and tried to leave.

'I don't want to come in,' he said. 'I was just playing knock-down Ginger.'

Uncle Eugene didn't believe him.

'I'm not stupid,' he said. 'I'm ill – I've poisoned myself. Never mix meths with Mogadon.'

'OK. I won't. Want me to call Dad?'

'No!' moaned Uncle Eugene. 'Don't you dare!'

Adam made him a cup of black coffee and, showing no mercy, pulled out his rocket drawing. Uncle Eugene held it close to his eyes and squinted as if he was having trouble focusing, which he was.

'What's *this* meant to be?'

'It's my school project.'

Adam explained in great detail, describing the materials he was thinking of using and how, if he failed, he'd never get into a decent secondary school and would end up being a drop-out like Sonny.

'And your father! And your father's father!' grumbled Uncle Eugene.

Eugene and Chas were twins, but apart from the fact that they were both going identically bald at the front, they had nothing in common.

They were the youngest of six brothers, and while Chas, Uncle Cliff, Uncle Lenny, Uncle Alf and Uncle Jed were all delighted to have achieved no formal qualifications and enjoyed working in the funfair with Granddad Clem and Grandma Marina, Uncle Eugene had other ambitions.

He'd set his sights somewhat higher than the helter-skelter. To his family's shame, he passed all his exams with flying colours and went to university. He loved it there. He was their brightest star. His nickname was Eugenius.

Sadly, he didn't become an astrophysicist, which had been the original plan. For reasons he could never articulate without setting off a painful spasm in his neck, he'd decided to become a teacher.

'Why, oh, why did I do that, Adam?' he wailed.

'How should I know, Uncle Eugene?'

He'd applied for a post in one of those secondary schools nobody wants to send their children to, dreaming of giving the Unfortunate Ones hope and raising them out of the mire.

'Those boys were the spawn of the devil! And the girls were even *worse*.'

He'd hated every minute of it. He'd stuck it out until he'd

had so many ink pellets thrown at him, it was impossible to see the original colour of his jacket.

Neither the jacket nor Uncle Eugene ever fully recovered. He'd visited a psychiatrist but it didn't help. Uncle Eugene thought the psychiatrist was a half-wit and accused him of asking too many personal questions.

Finally, he was persuaded to take early retirement. It helped, but not a lot. Since then, his moods swang from manic happiness to morbid despair. In his jollier moments, he would begin elaborate projects in his home laboratory where he would try, for example, to turn gold into lead, just to be awkward.

He'd be at it for days, completely forgetting to eat or sleep or take his pills. When it all went wrong, as it inevitably did, he would sweep the test tubes off the bench with his elbow. Then, like a mad chef, he would throw together a suicidal soup of chemicals, knowing full well they would make him choke, puke or blow his windows out.

Today, he was melancholy, but mellow. He was too weak for physical violence. He turned Adam's picture of the rocket upside down.

'It'll never get off the ground,' he muttered.

'Why not, Uncle Eugene?'

Just as Adam had hoped, he told him exactly why.

'Your average electric propulsion engine is a non-starter,' he said. 'It wouldn't give the rocket enough thrust to get off the ground.'

'Why not?'

Uncle Eugene sat up properly, took out a pencil and sucked the end thoughtfully.

'Too much air resistance,' he wheezed. 'It'd work fine in orbit round the earth because it would be almost weightless. You could try one engine to launch it and one for use in space I suppose, but there again – weight problems.'

He stirred his coffee with his pencil then prodded Adam's drawing with the wet end.

'What's this bit supposed to be? A jelly mould?'

'No, it's a motorbike engine. The teacher said to use stuff you found lying around. I found this crate full of . . .'

Uncle Eugene flapped his hand impatiently. 'Yes, yes. Stop wittering. I'm trying to think.'

He seemed to be going into a trance. He half-closed his eyes and slid down his chair, his head lolling about somewhere near the seat. Adam clicked his fingers in front of his face to check he hadn't died. Suddenly, Uncle Eugene's eyes sprang open and he heaved himself up by the armrests.

'There is *something* one could mix with petrol to give the rocket the extra oomph it needs . . .'

He trailed off, his eyes flickering wildly across a row of heavily thumbed chemistry textbooks that were causing his bookshelf to warp. He chose one and waved it at Adam enthusiastically.

'Stay there,' he commanded. 'I'm going to put some trousers on. I've had a thought.'

He disappeared down the narrow hallway with a definite spring in his step. Adam leant back in his chair and smiled.

Suddenly, there was an overpowering stench of rancid mince and wet carpet. Helium had entered the room. He waddled over to Adam and stuffed his flea-bitten head in his crotch, hoping to have his ears scratched.

Adam stood up pointedly and sat in another chair, but Helium wouldn't leave him alone. He jumped onto his lap, gazed into his eyes and then without warning, licked him slowly from his chin to his eyebrows. It was like having his face wiped with a piece of raw liver. Adam grabbed a cushion, held it firmly in front of his head and swore at Helium through the stuffing.

After a while, the dog jumped down. Adam took the cushion away and realized Uncle Eugene had come back. He'd heard every four-letter word.

'You *nasty* piece of work!' he said. 'You've hurt Helium's feelings!'

'I wasn't swearing *at* him, I was swearing *with* him. It was a game,' Adam insisted.

Uncle Eugene lightened up. 'Oh? Who won?'

'He did.'

'Did he? Good. Now then, this business with the rocket . . .'

Uncle Eugene licked his pencil and started to scribble all over Adam's plan.

'Let's assume all you had access to was a motorbike engine. The carburettor normally feeds a mixture of air and petrol into the motor, agreed?'

Adam nodded.

'Ordinary petrol wouldn't work, because there's no air in space,' Uncle Eugene continued. '*But* . . . if one could invent a powder that dramatically boosted the fuel and created oxygen in the process, you might just get somewhere.' Adam was taking notes.

'I see. So, you'd just mix this powder into the petrol? How would you know how much to use?'

'Trial and error,' replied Uncle Eugene. 'You'd have to do a test launch. If the formula is right, the exhaust gases should be pokey enough to launch the thing.'

Helium was lying on his back with his head on one side, drooling onto the rug. It gave Adam an idea.

'The Russians sent a dog up to test one of their rockets, didn't they?'

Uncle Eugene glared at him.

'We are not the Russians!' he barked. 'I forbid you to launch Helium into space.'

'OK. But could my rocket carry a large dog? Theoretically, I mean? The teacher is bound to want to know.'

If anything, Skippy weighed less than Helium, but there was all his equipment to consider. He'd have to borrow the bathroom scales and weigh it all.

'Theoretically? Yes, easily, I should think,' admitted Uncle Eugene. 'You must promise me you'll never *man* this rocket though.'

An alien wasn't a man, was it?

'I promise, Uncle Eugene.'

Now all Adam had to do was persuade him to invent the magic powder.

'Why should I?' said Uncle Eugene. 'What's it worth?'

'Two pounds fifty?'

Adam showed him the money his mother had given him to look after Fay.

'Is that it? Haven't you got anything in your other pocket?'

He showed him Twonk.

'Oh, for heaven's sake,' groaned Uncle Eugene. 'That's pathetic.'

He'd already made up his mind to do it anyway.

Adam walked back from Uncle Eugene's feeling very optimistic. The rocket project was under way. True, there were still a few minor technical hurdles to get over, like how to navigate the thing, but he felt sure Uncle Eugene would overcome them.

He also felt sure that once Skippy saw the rocket coming together, he might chip in with a few ideas of his own. After all, he was the expert. He was also the only one who knew how much fuel he'd need to get back to his planet. So far, he hadn't mentioned his address.

Adam wandered across the shingle towards The Black Hole, wondering if Fay had managed to teach the alien any new words. A sudden shout made him look up.

'*Aeroplan*! *Aeroplan*!'

Skippy was standing with his arms outstretched, his toes hanging right over the edge of the cliff. Below him was a thirty-foot drop.

Fay was seeing if he could fly.

Chapter Five

By rights, Skippy should have fallen to his death. Just as
Adam climbed high enough to reach out and grab him, he'd
flinched and slipped over the edge. There was no scream.
Adam waited for the sound of his body smashing against the
rocks below, but it never came.

With his heart in his mouth, he looked over. At first, he
couldn't see Skippy and it crossed his mind that he might
have vaporized. Who knew the extent of his cosmic tricks?

He could see Fay. She was jumping up and down excitedly
on the shingle, pointing up at a stony outcrop a short drop
below the place where Skippy had gone over.

'He's there! He flew into that gorse bush.'

She looked really pleased with herself.

'He *what*?'

It was hell getting down. Adam had to lower himself by his
arms and then side-step round a narrow, crumbling ledge.
Once, he almost lost his footing. Shaking and pale, he
crouched with his back pressed against rocks, which seemed
determined to push him off.

Skippy was hunched up in the middle of the gorse, flapping spastically like an injured bird. Adam couldn't tell if he
was hurt or not. He called out:

'Skippy, I'm here. Try and reach my hand!'

'Just let him fly down!' yelled Fay. 'He can do it.'

Skippy's forehead was punctured with thorns. Bright
beads of blood rolled down his face. Red blood, like Adam's.

'Come on, Skip. Don't be scared.'

Skippy wasn't scared in the slightest. Oblivious to his

wounds, he stood up on tiptoes, and looked into the sky, shielding his eyes from the glare of the sun. There was no sign of a rescue spaceship.

Adam leapt over a gap and landed next to him, stumbling and prickling his hand on the gorse as he tried to steady himself. He caught his breath and tried not to look down.

'I'm sure they'll be back for you soon, Skip. Which planet do they have to come from. Is it Mars? Venus?'

He doubted it was either. Mars was so cold. Venus was too hot. The temperature got up to 480 degrees sometimes. Adam pointed up at the clouds.

'Where do you live, Skippy?'

'Shquiperi . . . Evrope,' he said.

Evrope? Was he trying to tell him he came from Europa?

'What, one of the moons near Jupiter?'

Skippy nodded his head and took Adam's hand.

'Poshte julutem,' he muttered.

Juletem? Julutem! That must be his word for Jupiter!

'We're going to need an awful lot of petrol to get you home,' Adam sighed.

Fay was waiting for them at the bottom of the cliff. She seemed annoyed.

'Why didn't you let him fly down, Adam? You were the one who said not to treat him like a baby.'

He slapped her round the head. It wasn't a hard slap, but the shock of it made her cry out.

'What did you do that for? I haven't done anything wrong! It was meant to be a surprise.'

Adam hadn't meant to hit her. It was a reflex action, a kind of aftershock.

'Skippy can't fly,' he said.

'But *he can*! He's been practising all morning. He flew onto the ledge.'

Adam shook her by the shoulders.

'Fay, he fell! You nearly killed him.'

He pulled Twonk out of his pocket. Her face went white.

'Please, Adam. I didn't know!' she begged. 'I wouldn't do anything to hurt him.'

'You might by accident,' he said. 'As soon as I've fixed his rocket, he's going back to his planet.'

Her face fell.

'No! You don't even know where he lives!'

'I do. He comes from Julutem.'

Fay wiped her nose with the back of her hand.

'How long will it take to fix the rocket?'

Adam shrugged.

'A week, maybe.'

Fay's eyes filled with tears. A week was no time at all.

'But he might not want to go back. He likes it here! Adam, you can't send him back just to punish me. That's not fair.'

It wasn't to punish her, it was to save Skippy. But if that's how she chose to see it, it was all right by him. Hopefully, she'd hate him for it. That way, they could go back to the way things were. Feeling fond of Fay was a temporary blip. Once Skippy was gone, those feelings had to go too. They would have served their purpose.

'You're the one who's being selfish,' he told her. 'This isn't a game, Fay. Skippy's not a toy. You didn't really think he could stay here for ever, did you?'

Devastated by this cruel blow, she crawled into The Black Hole, curled up in a ball and cried.

*

Adam spent the rest of the afternoon in the cave, bolting rocket sections together. He'd take them apart later. Right now, he needed to make sure he'd got enough screws. Fay was still sulking and refused to help, but Skippy was more than happy to. He sat close to Adam, holding the tin of nuts and bolts. When Adam asked for one, he would pass it to him.

'Nut, please, Skippy.'

'Nut!'

Often he'd get the nuts and bolts muddled and Adam would have to remind him.

'This is a nut . . . *This* one's a bolt.' It took a long while to sink in.

'This nut?'

'No, that's a bolt, Skippy.'

'Bolt?'

'Yes. Pass me the bolt.'

'Nut?'

Fay thought it was hilarious and dried her eyes.

'Silly, isn't he?' she squealed.

'No! He can't be expected to pick up our language just like that.'

'Elephant!' smiled Skippy.

'I showed him my picture dictionary,' Fay explained. 'He can say all sorts, watch . . . What's this, Skippy?'

She pointed to her head.

'Nut!' he exclaimed.

Even Adam had to laugh.

'No!' said Fay. 'Head! On Planet Earth, we call it a head. Remember our song?'

She started to sing, doing all the actions, 'Heads and shoulders, knees and toes, knees and toes, knees and toes . . . join in, Skippy!'

Adam stared in disbelief as the little alien copied his sister in the nursery school ritual, chanting the words in pigeon English.

'We all clap hands to . . . gether!' sang Fay. 'Well done, Skippy! You're so clever.'

Adam shook his head in despair.

'He's just humouring you.'

*

Adam went home to get some more washers for the rocket fins. His father was bringing the motorbikes in from the front of the shop.

[58]

'All right, Ad? Where's Fay?'

'She's coming. She's just walking really slowly. She's really getting on my wick. Do I have to look after her tomorrow?'

'Well, Sonny can't, he's off to Knebworth. Have a look at Baby before he goes. She looks the business.'

'Can I have some washers, Dad?'

'Yeah, if you want.'

Adam was disappointed he hadn't asked what he wanted them for. He told him anyway.

'I'm making a model rocket for my school project. The person who makes the rocket fly highest gets extra points.'

'Yeah? That's good. What are you going to make it out of?'

To Adam's surprise, he actually sounded interested for once, but then Fay appeared.

'Hi, Daddy.'

'Hey, Princess!'

He picked her up and sat her on one of the bikes.

'Ride me into the shop, Dad!'

'All right, then. Holding on tight? Vrooom . . . vroom . . .'

Adam sighed and left them to it. He went up the back stairs and let himself into the flat. There was a fat brown envelope on the mat, addressed to him. There was no stamp, but he recognized the mad handwriting immediately. It was from Uncle Eugene.

Adam went to his bedroom, locked the door and tore open the envelope. Inside, there was a letter, several diagrams stapled together and one large plan, folded into four. His hands shook as he read the note:

> Adam, this is the best I can do for now, regarding your rocket project. Technically, it should work if you can get hold of the right bits of junk (see enclosed notes) but you might need Chas's help with some of it – e.g. fiddling around with the gear box etc . . .

Adam raced to the end of the letter, the most exciting part of which was the PS.

PS – I've almost cracked the formula to boost the petrol. Would have finished yesterday, only I suffered third-degree burns to my right thumb and was unable to agitate my flask.

Adam lay down on his bed and studied the diagrams carefully. On each sheet of paper, Uncle Eugene had drawn a different rocket section with numbered arrows pointing to notes.

On the first page, he'd designed a nose cone made from sheet metal. It had a window in it, made from a motorbike windscreen. This was to be sealed with Hermatite – there was a drawer full of that in the workshop. Chas used it to seal engines.

The next section was the cockpit, featuring a set of motorbike handlebars complete with gears, throttle and ignition. There was also a bike seat, which sat on a fuel tank. It looked remarkably like the seat on Sonny's bike. Uncle Eugene had added a note:

Even though this will be an un-manned flight, I've taken the liberty of adding a seat and an escape hatch for the imaginary pilot – it might earn you extra points for creativity.

Adam smiled to himself. Good old Uncle Eugene. Without knowing it, he'd created the perfect door for Skippy to exit through once he'd landed on Julutem.

Uncle Eugene had suggested using a motorbike engine to power the rocket – he'd drawn a cross-section of one, sitting inside a metal tube. It had been rotated through 90 degrees and bolted to a frame made from a couple of D-shaped lengths of pipe.

There was a set of universal joints, which attached the motor to the rotor inside the tube with the fins. The motor would make the rotor turn and when enough exhaust gases had built up, the rocket would lift off. That was the general idea, anyway. Adam was about to unfold the large plan when his door handle rattled.

'Adam, have you forgiven me yet?'

'No. Go away, Fay.'

He had forgiven her actually – he'd decided she was dopey rather than wicked. She really had believed Skippy could fly. She was sensible in a lot of ways, but she was still only six. She believed in Father Christmas and the Tooth Fairy. She hadn't the wit to calculate that Skippy's body mass and shape made it technically impossible for him to fly.

Forgiveness aside, he didn't want her interrupting him right now, not while he was trying to get his head round Uncle Eugene's calculations.

'I'm really sorry, Adam. Adam, I'll do anything you say. I was being stupid and selfish.'

He spread the large plan of the rocket out on the floor. It was a masterpiece. Definitely worth two pounds fifty of anybody's money. There was even a ready-made shopping list. This included everything from the number of screws he needed to suggestions of useful items to collect:

Item 6. Two large aerosol cans (e.g. for spray paint.) These would be ideal for making the hand-operated jets needed to steer the rocket.

Sonny had spray paint cans! Adam imagined Skippy shooting through time and space in a mist of Flame Orange. Fay knocked on the door again.

'I'll do anything you say, I *promise*. I'll even mend the spaceship.'

Adam let her in.

'Right!' he said, 'I want you to help me nick Sonny's bike.'

*

Having completed his test drive round the yard, Sonny dismounted and gave a growl of satisfaction. The weeks he'd spent re-building his bike had paid off. She was beautiful. He patted her saddle.

'Love you, Baby.'

His girlfriend, Bonita, stepped out of the shadows, scowling.

'You never say that to me. If you loved me, you'd take me to Knebworth tomorrow.'

'You're right,' said Sonny.

He lit a cigarette and leant back against the workshop door.

'So can I come?'

'No.'

She yanked the keys out of the ignition and threw them on the floor. Sonny called her a bitch. She turned on her high heels and clattered off, waiting for him to call her back, but he didn't. Adam could see tears running down her face. He was hiding behind the wheelie bins with Fay. In his backpack were a hacksaw, some extra blades and a cordless drill.

'Now?' whispered Fay.

They'd rehearsed what they were going to do. Fay had to distract Sonny back into the flat before he had a chance to lock Baby up for the night. Adam would then steer the motorbike through the back and down the alleyway. When he was out of earshot, he'd take her off-road through the spinney and wheel her down to the beach.

He couldn't believe his luck when Bonny threw the keys on the floor. If he could grab them, he could drive Baby there! He pushed Fay into the yard.

'*Now!*'

She began to wail at the top of her voice hysterically, 'Sonny, come quick . . . leeeeee!'

Her drama lessons were really paying off. She looked terrified. Sonny stubbed his fag out.

'Whassup, Princess? Why aren't you sleepybyes?'

'The python's escaped. He's in m . . . my bed! I called Adam but he's at Uncle Eugene's and Daddy's gone to the chip shop!'

Sonny shuddered visibly. Fay grabbed his arm and dragged him across the yard.

'It tried to strangle me! I was so scared, Sonny. Get it out of my bed! Get it *out*!'

It had taken Fay and Adam ages to settle the python under her duvet. They'd managed to carry it between them and fed it in through the pillow end, but it kept popping out again. Eventually, they trapped its head in her pyjama case and it stopped moving and went to sleep.

The 'escaping' python had been Adam's idea, of course. There were other methods he could have chosen, but knowing how much Sonny loathed that snake, this way was the sweetest.

Sonny picked Fay up in his arms and walked off.

'It's OK. Shhh. I've got you.'

There was a certain reluctance in his stride. Fay grinned at Adam over Sonny's shoulder then screamed at him to get a move on.

'Run, Sonny, *run!*'

As soon as they'd gone, Adam crept out from behind the bins, grabbed the ignition keys and kicked Baby's stand away. He hadn't realized how heavy she was and almost twisted her on to the floor.

In the end, he grabbed one of the high bars at the base, put his head through the middle and with his other hand on the gas tank managed to roll her into the alleyway out of sight.

Riding Baby was a lot harder than he thought. Although he could reach the foot pegs, his legs weren't long enough to reach the floor. The bike tipped easily and had thrown him off twice. Once, when he hit a log and again when he skidded on the shingle.

He hadn't realized how fast the acceleration was either. He'd driven Ghetto's Vespa round the yard lots of times, but compared to Baby, the Vespa was like an electric wheelchair. When he started her up in the woods, she slipped through his thighs and raced off without him.

By the time he got to The Black Hole he was a covered in

cuts and bruises and Baby wasn't much better.

Skippy was asleep when he got there. Adam tucked his free hand under the blanket and loosened the belt strap just a little on his left wrist. He looked so peaceful, he decided not to wake him. Dreaming of Julutem, no doubt.

Adam went back outside. There was no one around. He ran his fingers across the fresh blade in his hacksaw.

'Sorry, Baby but it's for a very good cause,' he explained, 'and it's going to hurt Sonny a whole lot more than it'll hurt you.'

With that happy thought in his head, he hacked her to bits.

*

Sonny didn't come down for breakfast.

'He's been crying, hasn't he, Daddy?' said Fay.

Chas nodded. His mouth was full of toast and he had marmalade in his beard.

'Why?' asked Adam innocently. 'Bonny dumped him?'

Chas shook his head.

'Baby's been half-inched.'

Adam pretended to be mortified.

'*Stolen?* Who would do such a terrible thing?'

Fay pushed her face into her glass of milk. Adam could tell by her eyebrows she was trying not to laugh.

'I only nipped out for five minutes to get some chips and she'd gone,' sighed Chas.

Adam kicked Fay in the leg to help her get a grip.

'Did they break into the workshop, Dad?'

'No, Sonny never had a chance to lock her up. The python escaped. What time did you get back, by the way?'

Adam shrugged.

'Tennish? I was round Uncle Eugene's.'

'Uncle Eugene's helping him make a stupid rocket,' Fay added, sarcastically. 'In any case, you were supposed to be looking after me, Adam. Mum said.'

They started to argue, but then Sonny came in and the room fell silent.

'Whoever did it dies.'

Chas poured him a cup of tea.

'I don't want tea, I want my effin' bike back!' Sonny yelled. He put his head in his hands.

'Sonny said the "E" word,' whispered Fay.

Chas offered to lend Sonny another bike from the shop.

'You can have any one you like, Son. I know it's not the same, but at least you can still go to Knebworth with The Cast-offs.'

Sonny lifted his head slowly. 'The *Outcasts*!' he snarled, thumping the table.' And I don't want *another* bike. I want *my* bike. All the other bikes are crap.'

Chas looked rather hurt.

'What . . . all of them?'

Sonny picked the teapot-stand up and hurled it across the room like a discus. By sheer fluke, it flew straight out of the window. Adam hooted into his cornflakes. Fay slid under the table. Sonny's face was scarlet with rage.

'Don't you *dare* laugh, Dweeb.'

But he wasn't the only one. Chas had pulled his beard up over his lips to stifle his guffaws. Sonny stormed out.

'I'm glad you all think it's so funny, you bunch of losers!'

He did go to Knebworth in the end. Slash and Ghetto persuaded him to borrow Chas's Harley Panhead. It was twice as old as him and not a patch on Baby, but Sonny was in the mood for a fight, and this bike had seen several. They were well matched.

Chas, Adam and Fay stood on the pavement and waved The Outcasts off. Afterwards, Chas picked up the teapot-stand, which was lying in the road and asked Adam to take Fay to her Kung Fu class.

'I don't *want* to go to Kung Fu,' she insisted.

'Mummy wants you to go to Kung Fu.'

Fay stamped her foot.

[65]

'How come I have to go to Kung Fu and Adam doesn't?'

'Mum loves you more,' Adam reminded her.

Paris Williams's mother was going to pick Fay up after her class, so Adam had the whole day to himself.

He spent a productive morning in The Black Hole surrounded by bits of Baby. He drilled and bolted and sawed until his hands were raw. He'd stuck Uncle Eugene's diagrams to the cave wall and explained them all carefully to Skippy. He'd given him a pencil.

'Make any changes you want,' he said. 'This is your rocket.'

Skippy had made a series of careful dots and dashes on the cockpit. Adam couldn't interpret them, but he assumed they were to do with navigation.

Uncle Eugene thought it would be possible to fit one of those satellite systems made for boats – all they'd have to do was replace the road map with a star map. Only he didn't say how.

'Don't worry, Skippy. We'll sort something out.'

He put it on his long list of 'Things to ask Uncle Eugene'.

He was dying to go round there to see if the fuel-booster powder was ready.

Chapter Six

By the end of the week, the rocket was almost finished. Chas had let him have all sorts of hardware, including the sheet metal for the nose cone and Baby's old windscreen. Unfortunately, he would keep asking questions. If this was the size of the window, how big was the rocket going to be? Adam told him about two metres long. But it was bigger.

'Two metres! How are you gonna get it to school? It won't fit on the bus.'

'We don't have to bring all of it in,' Adam explained.

Chas wasn't convinced. 'Why not?'

'Like you said. It's too big. The important thing is the diagram and the calculations.'

Just when Adam thought he was out of the woods, Chas offered to let him make the rocket in his workshop. There was plenty of space now Sonny had finished Babe.

'No, it's all right, Dad. I'm making it at a friend's house. We're doing it between us.'

'Which friend?'

Adam nearly said Moses.

'M . . . ark. He's got this really massive bedroom.'

He persuaded Chas to part with the switches off his bench drill and got him to explain how to wire them up from the cockpit to the outside of the rocket. He'd realized yesterday with a horrid jolt that he'd never be able to launch it unmanned unless he could start it up from the outside.

Now he had a set of on-off switches he could wire straight into the ignition. All he'd have to do was press the red button to start the engine.

'Thanks, Dad.'

'That's all right, mate. Nice to have some time together. We haven't really talked since you were about three, have we? Why's that then, Ad?'

'I couldn't get a word in edgeways. And you like Sonny more.'

Chas went pink.

'No, I don't.'

Adam knew he was lying by the way he kept fiddling with his ponytail. He let him sweat for a bit, then:

'Got any string, Dad?'

'String? Got loads of string. How much do you want?'

Adam needed it to tie down the clutch and the throttle, being as there'd be no pilot to operate them on the test flight. Chas unravelled far more than necessary, as if the generosity of the extra string was proof of his endless love for his second boy.

'Go on, son. Take it. There, have a bit more!'

Armed with his switches and string, Adam went back to The Black Hole to put the finishing touches to the rocket. All he had to do now was wire in the switches, bolt the sections together, add Uncle Eugene's powder to the fuel and stand well back.

Uncle Eugene had been extremely excited when Adam rode round to see if he'd managed to crack the formula for the fuel.

'Oh, yes!' he'd whooped. 'I could sell this stuff to terrorists and make an absolute killing.' He ushered Adam into his makeshift chemical factory and held up a flask of yellow powder.

'I call it Trizone X,' he announced. '"Tri" meaning triple the power and "zone" referring to its remarkable oxygen-producing capability.'

'What does the "X" stand for?' asked Adam. 'Explosive?'

Uncle Eugene pursed his lips. 'I'm not telling you. It's a state secret.'

Adam refused to beg him for it. Uncle Eugene was unbearable when he was cocky.

'Thanks, Uncle Eugene.'

Just as he was about to leave with the precious powder weighed into a silver tin, Uncle Eugene dropped a bomb.

'Can I come to the test launch, please?'

It seemed unfair not to let him. It was mostly his project after all. Without him, there would be no rocket. But he couldn't let him catch sight of Skippy. No, no, no – Uncle Eugene was as desperate as Adam to be the brightest star in the world of space exploration. If he got the slightest whiff of an alien, he'd have no qualms about exposing it and would go out of his way to steal his nephew's glory. He'd push him under a bus if necessary.

'Sorry, I'm afraid it's not allowed, Uncle Eugene.'

'Nonsense. Who says?'

'School rules,' Adam insisted. 'If they know you helped me with the project, I'll never get extra points. I might even get expelled for cheating.'

Uncle Eugene went ballistic. He was going to write to the school and complain. Something as dangerous as launching a rocket shouldn't be allowed without adult supervision.

'You know my friend Mark? His dad's going to supervise,' lied Adam. 'He teaches at my school, he's going to be in charge of the test launches.'

Uncle Eugene narrowed his eyes.

'How many rockets are there? How many children in your class? Thirty-two?'

There were thirty-one, now Moses had left. Uncle Eugene wouldn't let the matter drop.

'Thirty-one rockets? Mark's dad's spreading himself a bit thinly, isn't he?'

'There's less than that,' Adam insisted. 'We're making them in teams. We're setting them all off at once from the playground.'

'*Armageddon*!' squeaked Uncle Eugene, pushing his fingers and thumbs into his ears, eyes and nostrils as if to prevent his brain oozing out of the holes. He deliberately nutted his head against the door then advanced on Adam, prodding him in the chest with his biro.

'Right! Fair enough. Off you go! Let's hope "Marks's Dad" knows what he's doing. I bet he hasn't even got a degree. I bet he went to art college! Got an earring, has he?'

The plastic refill shot out of his pen. He batted Adam away, unable to hide his mounting jealousy of non-existent Mark's non-existent dad.

'I'll take a photo,' Adam promised as he backed away. 'For you to keep.'

Small comfort. Uncle Eugene clearly felt he was being short-changed. He rolled up the charred sleeve on his laboratory coat and began to flex his elbow.

Any second now, he was going to sweep all his test tubes off the table.

*

Adam went straight from Uncle Eugene's to Paris Williams's house to pick up his sister. He didn't want to, but he'd promised Fay she could help him test-launch the rocket. Much as he wanted to do it all by himself, an extra pair of hands would come in useful – he just wished they were Commander Shoderu's hands instead of hers.

Paris answered the door dressed as a bride.

'Hello, Adam! Are you going down to the beach? Can I come?'

'No. We're just going home.'

Fay came downstairs in an ill-fitting bridesmaid's outfit and refused to move.

'Adam, you promised we could go to the beach!'

'Dad wants you in the shop. Hurry up. Put your shoes on.'

She stuck her bottom lip out.

'But you promised!'

He patted his back pocket menacingly. 'Oooh . . . what's in my pocket? Is it a little donkey?'

Reluctantly, Fay changed back into her proper clothes and went with him, moaning non-stop. Although she'd agreed to help with the rocket, she still couldn't accept that Skippy had to leave. She felt powerless and angry.

'You're a horrible liar, Adam! How come I have to stay in the shop and you don't?'

'Dad loves you more.'

'No, he doesn't. He loves Sonny more.'

Fay was so busy sulking, it took her some time to realize they weren't going back to Lurie's Motors after all.

'Where are we going? Are we going to the beach?'

'What does it look like, dummy?'

Fay grabbed Adam's hand and kissed it.

'Oh, brilliant! Why didn't you say?'

'Ugh. Get off.' He snatched his hand away. 'If Paris knew we were going to the beach, she'd want to come too. We don't want anyone to see the rocket, Fay. They'll stop us launching it. You don't want to ruin it for Skippy, do you?'

She certainly didn't. But he shouldn't have said what he did. It had given her an idea.

Skippy was in a very good mood when they arrived at The Black Hole. Adam had taken him some breakfast earlier, before he went round to Uncle Eugene's – a fried egg he'd saved from his own breakfast and some fruit. When he left, Skippy was sitting on the lilo stroking a peach.

'Tungytatta, Skippy!' called Fay.

The rocket lay in three sections on the cave floor. Skippy was sitting in the cockpit holding onto the handlebars and opening the throttle.

'See? He knows how to operate it,' said Adam. 'You can't be the pilot today though, Skippy. We need to test it unmanned.'

Skippy was reluctant to get out, but Adam needed to put the Trizone X into the fuel tank and bolt everything together.

'Can you move please, Skip? I need you to help me with the nuts and bolts.'

Skippy stayed exactly where he was.

'Nuts and bolts!' he said. He had no sense of urgency at all. Adam sighed and decided to work round him. Fay helped him carry the fin section over to the shingle. It was hard going.

'The engine section is even heavier,' puffed Adam. 'I'll have to make a go-kart or we'll never get it up the cliff. Can I have the wheels off your doll's pram?'

'Um . . . OK.' She wrinkled her nose and shrugged. 'Doll's prams are babyish, anyway.'

Adam wasn't going to do the test launch from the cliff. If it went wrong, the rocket would be smashed to pieces. Apart from that, someone might see them. People occasionally walked their dogs round there. He would set the rocket up behind the groyne.

He ordered Fay to fetch a blanket and some rope from The Black Hole. She asked what he wanted them for.

'I'm going to hang you with the rope and hide your body in the blanket.'

'If you do that, I won't give you my pram wheels,' warned Fay.

'All right. I need the rope to tether the rocket so it doesn't shoot off until there's enough thrust and I need the blanket to cover it up in case anyone comes. Satisfied?'

Fay trotted back to The Black Hole. Skippy was still sitting in the cockpit. She sat on the fuel tank and put her arms round him.

'Out you get, Skippy. We need you to come and help us.'

He rubbed his cheek against hers, like a friendly cat.

'Peach,' he said.

'You don't really want to go home, do you?' she sighed. 'You like it here with me.'

*

By six o'clock that evening, the rocket was ready. It was tethered with two long ropes; one attached to an iron loop in the side of the groyne, the other round a heavy boulder a

[72]

good distance up the beach.

'What if it zooms into outer space and you lose it?' asked Fay, hopefully.

'Uncle Eugene said if I angle the nose cone and only use a teaspoon of Trizone X, it should only go a little way out to sea,' Adam told her. 'It's the height that's important.'

Fay thought for a moment.

'How will you get it back?'

He'd already worked that one out.

'The tide will bring it in. We can pull it ashore with the tether ropes.'

It would have been better if they could have waited until dark, but it was summer. By the time proper darkness fell, Chas would be wondering where they were.

'We could go home for tea and then come out again,' Fay suggested brightly.

'What if someone sees the rocket while we're at the flat, dopey?'

Despite the blanket, it was a very large object to hide. Fay folded her arms crossly.

'I was only *saying*. What do *you* think we should do, if you're so clever?'

Adam looked along the length of the beach. Up at the cliffs. There was no one around.

'Launch it now,' he said.

He pulled the blanket away and with a pounding heart, began to whisper under his breath. 'This is Captain Lurie to Starflight Commander Shoderu. We have the all-clear to launch. Do you read me?'

'*I read you, Captain. Go ahead. Good luck! Over.*'

'Who are you taking to?' asked Fay.

Adam blushed.

'No one. Stand right back. No, *further!* Beyond the end of the ropes. Take Skippy with you! Ten-nine-eight-seven-six –'

Fay couldn't bear the suspense. 'Adam, hurry up!'

He climbed onto a rock and pressed the red button on the

[73]

side of the cockpit. Nothing happened. His heart sank. Maybe there was a loose connection between the starter button and the pilot's consul.

'Doesn't it work?' Fay called brightly. 'I didn't think it would. Hooray!'

He ignored her and pressed the button hard with his thumb. The engine coughed as if it was clearing its throat then began turning over. Adam yanked away the string that was holding the throttle open, leapt down on to the shingle and sprinted back to safety. He pulled his knife out, ready to slash through the tethers.

Blue smoke curled up from the base of the rocket. Skippy was the first to spot it and began to pace up and down excitedly. Adam had gone into a world of his own:

'This is Captain Lurie to Commander Shoderu. We have achieved maximum thrust. Do you agree? Over.'

'This is Commander Shoderu. Maximum thrust achieved, Captain. Prepare to launch the rocket. Over.'

The rumbling from the engine was phenomenal. Fay was hopping about with her hands over her ears. Skippy was copying her. The rocket rattled like a giant washing machine with a ton of loose change caught in the drum.

Adam sliced frantically through one rope. The rocket was straining to get away. He was about to cut the other rope when it whipped out from under its boulder, slapped him round the back of the head and shot into the sky behind the soaring rocket. Adam slapped the shingle ecstatically.

'Whoah! Did you see *that*!!'

Fay and Skippy were staring up at the clouds, their mouths hanging open. Suddenly, their expressions changed. The rocket was heading for France!

'Agh . . . No! Come back!'

Adam ran towards the sea, waving his arms in the thin hope he could attract the attention of the invisible pilot, praying for him to change course. Suddenly, the engine went silent. Adam stared in disbelief as the rocket dropped from the sky and landed belly-up in the sea as if it had been shot. He kicked off his shoes.

'I'm going in!'

'Don't! It's too far out!' yelled Fay.

Either he wouldn't listen or he couldn't hear. The rocket was bobbing up and down about a hundred metres away. He wasn't a great swimmer, he hadn't had lessons like Fay, but he could easily do that in the swimming pool.

However, the sea was nothing like a swimming pool. Although the tide was coming in, there was a nasty undercurrent near the groyne and despite the good weather, it was icy cold. Adam powered along for the first fifty metres but then a mixture of tiredness and terror began to creep over him. He kept telling himself if he could grab hold of one of the tether ropes, he'd be fine – he could use it to pull himself up onto the rocket and float back.

Something gripped his leg like a vice. Cramp! He pinched his calf to ease the pain, but all that did was tip him off balance.

'Help!'

There was no shallow end to swim to, no lifeguard to call, no reassuring rail to grab.

'Hel . . . p!'

He tried treading water with his good leg, but a big wave smacked him so hard in the mouth he couldn't breathe. He lost co-ordination and sucked the stinging water right into his nostrils. He swallowed some, the rest ended up in his lungs. Now he was unable to call out. Every time he coughed, the effort sent him back under the water. He felt a dull pain on the side of his head then everything went black.

*

If it hadn't been for Fay, Adam would have drowned. She'd seen him in trouble from the beach and being the youngest member of Puddle Ducks Swimming Club to hold a silver medal, she knew he was drowning, not waving.

'You stay there, Skippy!'

At first, she thought about running back to The Black Hole to fetch the lilo, but there wasn't time. Stripping down to her underwear, she knotted up her cotton trousers and whirled them round so that they filled with air. Using this as a float, she battled her way across the waves like a small, blonde shrimp.

She could see Adam struggling in the water and called out to him, but he hadn't seen her. She was about four metres away when a massive wave sent the floating rocket forwards, cracking him on the head. He began to slide under the surface.

The sea was so murky, she wouldn't have been able to find him if he'd gone under. Luckily, the back of his sweatshirt had become hooked over a bolt, suspending him with his mouth a fraction above the water. This gave her just enough time to grab him before the next wave dislodged him.

Standing on one of the fins, she managed to heave Adam up onto the rocket. He flopped down onto his stomach, vomited and called for his mother. He was so surprised to see Fay, he nearly fell back into the sea.

'You shouldn't be here!' he shivered. 'It's dangerous!'

As they floated slowly back to shore, Adam seemed more concerned that Fay was only wearing her pants and vest rather than the fact that he'd nearly died.

'I saved your life, Ugly,' she reminded him.

'No, you never!'

'Yes, I did!'

He knew she had. He was just deeply embarrassed by the fact. It was asking too much to say thank you, but he knew he owed her a big one.

He took Twonk out of his pocket, wrung him out and handed him back to Fay.

'Quits.'

He'd never seen anyone look quite as grateful and although he was shivering with cold, something melted in him.

Chapter Seven

There wasn't too much damage to the rocket. By the time Adam had carried all the parts back to the cave, it was late. When they finally arrived home, Chas was pulling what was left of his hair out – What time did they call this? Why were their clothes all wet? Where the hell had they been?

'Swimming.'

'*Swimming?* At this time of night?'

Adam did his best to convince him.

'Well, when we say swimming, we were paddling. Fay fell in.'

'I fell in,' agreed Fay.

Chas said neither of them could be trusted. Mum was coming home the next night, they could spend tomorrow tidying their rooms and cleaning the flat.

Neither of them protested. They knew from experience they'd only have to be a little bit good and he'd let them off the hook. He'd be too busy in the shop to stick to his parental guns. Fay was worried though.

'What about Skippy, Adam? Who will unstrap him?'

'I will. I'll say the python needs a mouse and I have to go to the pet shop.'

Next day, Adam got up early, gave Chas tea in bed and fed him the pet shop story. Chas swallowed it, grunted and went back to sleep, so he jumped on his bike, raced to The Black Hole and sorted Skippy out.

Skippy was keen to polish the rocket, but there wasn't a dry cloth available so Adam lent him one of his socks to use instead.

'I'll be back a soon as I can. I've been grounded,' he explained.

Skippy was so absorbed with his buffing, he didn't care if Adam was there or not, so he pedalled back home at break-neck speed and by the time his dad came down, he was busily cleaning out the snake.

After that, he tidied his bedroom. Or rather, he threw everything that was on the floor into a cupboard.

Fay was far creepier. She put a frilly apron on and used so much cleaning spray, the room misted up.

'Haven't I done it nicely, Daddy?' she beamed.

'Lovely,' he choked. 'I think that's enough polishing now, don't you?'

She asked if Paris Williams could come round to play.

'We'll just play tea parties. You won't have to make us any-thing to eat. We'll just have cheese cut into dolly cubes.'

By the time Paris arrived, Adam had wangled permission to visit Uncle Eugene. Chas was serving in the shop at the time.

'It's not like I'm going round there to have fun, is it, Dad? I'm doing it out of duty. Think of it as part of my punish-ment.'

'Yeah, all right. Off you go.'

He wasn't even listening.

After getting no response from repeatedly banging the door knocker, Adam climbed in through Uncle Eugene's bedroom window. He flung open his curtains, announced he'd test-launched the rocket and told him that Mark's father had brought his motorboat along, in case the rocket went far out to sea.

Uncle Eugene sat up in bed, exposing Helium who was snoring snottily under the covers, and stopped him right there.

'Motorboat? Mark's father sounds very well off for a teacher. Big house? Motorboat? Has he won the lottery?'

[78]

'He bets on the horses,' Adam explained.

Uncle Eugene picked his nose and stared into space.

'Did you manage to get the rocket off the ground between you?'

The way Adam told it, the rocket had only gone up a few miserable feet and barely made it to the sea.

'It was very disappointing,' he lied.

Uncle Eugene looked perplexed. He began to fire questions at him, scribbling down the answers on the back of the *Radio Times*. What kind of noise did the rocket make when it started up? How long was it physically in the air before the engine cut out? What ratio of fuel to Trizone X had he used?

Adam didn't want to play it down, but this rocket had to take Skippy back to Julutem – that was a whole lot further than France. Trizone X was powerful, but frankly, Adam felt Uncle Eugene was holding back with the more lethal chemicals in the responsible way teachers do.

Uncle Eugene shook his head.

'I can't believe it only went that far. By my calculations, we should have created quite a dangerous missile. Oh, well.'

'Oh *well*? Isn't there anything you can do?' exclaimed Adam. 'There must be! You went to university. There's another boy in my class – Billy . . . Billy Tadger? His dad's only a greengrocer and his rocket went so far it hasn't even come back yet!'

Uncle Eugene wasn't about to be beaten by a greengrocer. He leapt out of bed, put his lab coat over his underpants and marched over to his chemical collection.

'Greengrocer, eh?'

He snapped on a pair of stained latex gloves.

'We'll see who knows their onions!'

He picked up a sealed bottle and unscrewed the lid. The contents began to glow.

*

Adam decided to leave Uncle Eugene to it. He had a lot to do today. For a start, he needed to make a go-cart to carry the rocket to the top of the cliff. Fay was in the kitchen with Paris, raiding the fridge.

'Can I have your pram wheels?' he asked.

'Make him say please,' said Paris. 'Otherwise it's rude.'

Adam rolled his eyes and groaned. '*Pleeeeeease.*'

Paris giggled at him. He couldn't stand Paris Williams. She reminded him of a meringue – sickly-sweet and full of air. He smiled at her nastily.

'Oh shut up, little girl.'

Fay put her head on one side.

'Are you going to the beach today, Adam?'

'No. I'm going to make a go-kart; then I'm going to Uncle Eugene's.'

'Will you be out all afternoon?'

'Prob'ly. Why?'

He was looking for a particular screwdriver in the kitchen drawer, so he didn't notice her exchange glances with Paris Williams.

'I just wondered.'

He found Fay's doll's pram and wheeled it into the yard. Chas was changing a tyre on a Suzuki. He saw Adam and laughed.

'Who's the mother?'

'What?'

'Get you, taking dolly for a nice walk.'

Adam went scarlet and let go of the pram handle.

'I'm *not*. I need it to make a go-cart.'

'Icy calm. I was only having a laugh. I'll give you a hand if you like.' Chas looked at his watch. 'I'm closing for lunch in a minute.'

Adam didn't need any help. He'd just built a working rocket. He could make a go-cart blindfolded. Still, it would save time if he had an assistant.

'OK,' he shrugged.

[80]

His dad tried to make conversation while he took the wheels off the pram.

'How was Uncle Eugene?'

'OK.'

Chas offered him a wooden bike crate to make the body of the cart.

'This any good to you?'

'OK.'

The crate was wide enough. Too deep if anything. He decided to saw it down. It needed to be as light as possible to get up the cliff path. He could tell Chas was watching him.

'So, Adam. How's your rocket project going with – who is it? Mark?'

'OK.'

He was going to take the rocket up the cliff in sections. They'd have to be strapped in. It would be a bumpy ride.

'Dad, have you got anything I can use for straps?'

'What do you want straps for, son?'

Adam tutted.

'In case I need to strap something in?'

'All right. Only asked. I'll shut up, shall I?' mumbled Chas. 'I'll be glad when Karen gets back. At least I'll have someone to talk to.'

'You never talk to Mum,' Adam pointed out. 'Why d'you think she's gone away?'

Chas went silent. He finished his fag and went back into the shop. Adam felt relieved, but confused. All those times he'd craved his attention – now it had been offered, he just wanted to be left alone.

Deep down, he didn't want the rocket to work. It was bound to, though. Uncle Eugene would see to that. Soon, Skippy would go back to his own kind and no one would ever know he'd been here. No one, except him and Fay. Was he right to keep it a secret? He was beginning to have his doubts.

Maybe he *should* tell an adult. Maybe something as rare and important as an alien should be preserved and studied by experts for the good of mankind, even if it meant sacrificing its freedom and happiness. Possibly its life.

Did an individual's happiness matter a jot in the greater scheme of things? He couldn't make up his mind. He almost wished something would happen to take the awful decision away, but a niggling voice kept reminding him he'd put so much effort into building the rocket it would be a great pity not to use it, and he was afraid this was swaying his judgement.

When he'd finished, Adam went through all the cupboards in the flat and loaded his backpack with provisions for Skippy. It was his last chance to take things freely before his mother came home.

He rode the go-kart round to Uncle Eugene's and parked it on the front lawn. As he went up the front path, his first thought was that Uncle Eugene's front window looked unusually clean. Then he realized there was no glass in it.

On closer inspection, the curtains were soaking wet and smudged with soot. There was a horrible smell of smoke and Helium was lying on the grass with his paws over his eyes. Helium never ventured outside unless there was an emergency.

'Uncle Eugene?'

There was no reply. Adam knocked so hard the knocker came off in his hand. He could hear a lot of swearing and shuffling, so he shouted through the letterbox.

'Open the door. It's me!'

Finally, it opened. There stood Uncle Eugene, minus eyebrows, eyelashes and most of his hair. His left hand was bandaged like a lollipop and the buttons on his lab coat had melted. He looked radiant.

'I've had a result,' he beamed.

*

After helping his uncle to clean up the worst of the fire damage, Adam set off with the little phial of Quinzone X swathed in several layers of bubble wrap.

[82]

'Whatever you do, don't spill it,' Uncle Eugene stressed. 'It'll combust. If you do cause an explosion, don't tell a living soul I gave it to you. You found it in a bin outside the British Legion. You don't know where I live.' He made Adam swear on his father's life.

'I swear.'

Compared to Quinzone X, Trizone X was about as deadly as Ribena. The new chemical was based on a similar formula, only this time Uncle Eugene had suspended it in alcohol, which increased its power by five. No one was more surprised than he was – he'd discovered its potential by accidentally knocking the remains of a tin of Trizone into the tumbler of absinthe he'd poured himself for breakfast.

'So, how far will the rocket travel on Quinzone X?' Adam asked casually.

There was a long pause. Uncle Eugene pressed his throbbing fingertips together and trying his best not to gloat, gave him the answer:

'A hell of a lot further than the greengrocer's!'

He'd given Adam so many warnings about the formula, he was beginning to wonder if he should be allowed to have it. He didn't want to put Skippy in any danger.

'It's perfectly safe once it's mixed with petrol,' Uncle Eugene insisted. 'You've got a ten-second safety margin between opening the phial and emptying the contents. In fact, I've got so much confidence in it, I might even try it out on my lawnmower.'

Adam looked at the charred remains of Uncle Eugene's clothing. His singed curtains. The brown, smoking hole in the rug.

'Please don't do that until I've gone,' he begged.

He turned to leave, but suddenly realized that if he went without saying anything, he'd reached the point of no return. He had everything he needed to launch the rocket now, except the moral justification. He needed to be reassured.

'Uncle Eugene, I've got a problem. Can I talk to you about it?'

'Is it to do with money?'

Uncle Eugene started to close his front door.

'No.'

'What then? Drugs? If it's sex, I don't want to know.'

'Ugh! Nor do I . . . can I come in?'

Uncle Eugene groaned.

'Oh all right then,' he snapped. 'But don't think you're getting a biscuit.'

'I don't want a biscuit,' Adam said. 'I want to know if you think one person's happiness and freedom is worth sacrificing for the sake of humanity.'

Uncle Eugene tutted loudly and sat down.

'Oh, It's going to be one of *those* conversations is it?' he sighed. 'Like a silly college debate, only with a . . . how old are you?'

'Ten. Nearly eleven.'

'Nearly eleven, and you want to know if one person's happiness should be sacrificed for the sake of . . .' he broke off. 'Who is this person with the happiness? I've never had any happiness! He should try living in my shoes.' He lifted his feet up and gazed at his blackened slippers. 'Burnt sacrifices!' he barked.

'If I make you a cup of tea, will you be serious?' asked Adam.

Uncle Eugene shook his head. 'I'm being perfectly serious. You've started me off, now sit there and suffer. This person that's up for sacrifice, is it anyone we know?'

'No,' said Adam, hastily. 'It isn't a person exactly. Look, say you found a unicorn . . . or . . . I don't know . . . an alien.' Here, he laughed aloud to throw Uncle Eugene off the scent, then continued, 'Do you think it would be best to look after it yourself and not tell anyone in case they hurt it . . . or should you hand it over to a zoo?'

'I don't know,' said Uncle Eugene. 'I've only ever looked after a dog.'

Adam felt Uncle Eugene was being deliberately evasive.

'All right then, say Helium was really, really rare . . .'

'I'm afraid he's rather common,' interrupted Uncle Eugene. 'That's why I called him Helium, after one of the most plentiful gases in the universe.'

'I thought you called him that because he farted a lot.'

'No. Why would I? Farts are mostly methane.'

Adam had completely lost his train of thought by now. Luckily, Uncle Eugene picked it up at the next station.

'Forget the rare dog business. I know what you're trying to get at. Look, what it boils down to is this – do you think the human race is worth saving?'

Adam thought about it. The people he hated easily outnumbered the few he liked.

'I dunno. Sonny's human, isn't he?'

Uncle Eugene scoffed, 'Is he? Is he that far up the evolutionary ladder? Not from where I'm standing.'

'Why's he so horrible to me, Uncle Eugene?'

'Because he's frightened. Intelligence frightens him, so he attacks! He has the IQ of a lesser primate – a baboon, for example. Imagine how threatened he must feel in the presence of a genius . . . and you *are* a genius, aren't you. Adam?'

He leant towards him and sucked his pipe noisily, right in his face. Adam didn't like to disagree in case he set fire to his nose.

'Yes, Uncle Eugene.'

'Then answer your *own* question! You don't need me to tell you how to think.'

He got up, opened the front door and ushered Adam out.

'May all your unicorns run free!' he cried, 'Up the unicorns! Up the aliens!'

The women over the road banged her window shut.

'Up yours, too, Uncle Eugene!' called Adam. 'Cheers!'

He had his answer now.

*

Thanks to the considerable speed of the go-cart, Adam reached the beach much earlier than he'd expected. He still had a large chunk of afternoon to himself to put the finishing details to the rocket. Apart from installing the navigation system, which Uncle Eugene had bought second-hand from *Hello Sailor Shipping Supplies*, there was a solar panel to attach. This had fallen off the new parking meter outside the library, straight into Uncle Eugene's shopping bag.

The solar panel was important. It would give the rocket the extra mileage it needed once the fuel had run out.

'I don't want anything for it,' Uncle Eugene had said. 'Except Mark's father's telephone number.'

'Fine,' said Adam, and gave him the wrong one.

He parked the go-cart outside The Black Hole, took his backpack off and stretched. It was a roasting afternoon. He pulled off his T-shirt and went into The Black Hole to greet Skippy.

'Tungytatta, Skip!'

He didn't answer, but there was nothing unusual in that. He was probably sitting in the rocket at the back of the cave and couldn't hear him. His hearing wasn't great. At least, he didn't respond terribly well to the pitch of Adam's voice. Sometimes, he tuned in to something much further away, way beyond Adam's earshot. Was it the music of the stars or a signal from Julutem? He wouldn't say. Whatever it was, it must have been beautiful or extremely important because it was impossible to distract Skippy when he was listening to it.

Adam checked the cockpit. He wasn't there. Maybe he was hiding? No, Skippy wasn't one for practical jokes. He was practical, full stop. He liked repetitive things. Sweeping or polishing or sorting objects into piles. He never tired of it. He was a good worker, always willing to help.

'Tungytatta, Skip?'

No reply. Where had he gone? He'd never wandered off on his own before. If Adam told him to stay somewhere, he stayed. Skippy obeyed him like a soldier obeys his superior.

He probably had military training. His strategy of Doing As He Was Told was his best means of defence on a strange planet.

Skippy did have a mind of his own, though. Sometimes, he would refuse to eat. At first, Adam thought he was being faddy, but then it dawned on him; Skippy was actually being generous. If he thought the meagre offerings Adam brought were typical of an Earth meal, he might logically assume there was a food shortage on Earth and didn't want Adam to starve at his expense.

Say there was a famine on Julutem? He'd be used to saving water and eating next to nothing. He was certainly thin and he never washed. Maybe the reason he'd come on this mission was to see if Earth was a good place to bring his family, if his own planet was dying.

Adam was about to look for him outside when he spotted something familiar sticking out of the eiderdown on the lilo. It was Twonk. He gritted his teeth. Fay had been here on her own with Skippy. He'd told her never to do that.

Unfortunately, the truth was even worse; as Adam searched along the beach, he heard a familiar giggle, which could only belong to one person. He crept round the side of the cove, and there they all were: Skippy, Fay and *Paris Williams!*

They were having a tea party.

*

Adam didn't lose his temper straight away. He walked over to Fay, who clearly wasn't expecting him and showed her that he had custody of Twonk.

'Pack the picnic up.'

'But we haven't finished!' protested Paris.

'I think we probably have, Paris,' said Fay.

Paris wasn't sure what was going on, but she was aware of a nasty atmosphere and crammed the last of the cheese cubes into her mouth. Adam whipped the tablecloth out from under the doll's plates and cups and folded it up. He glared at Paris, who was trying to stare him out.

'Your mum's going to go nuts when she finds out you came here on your own, Paris.'

'Your mum's going to go nuts when she finds out about your alien,' she retorted.

Adam looked at Fay. Her face was red. She couldn't look him in the eye. He pulled Twonk out of his back pocket and started whirling him round by his tail. Fay panicked and grabbed a fistful of Paris's curls.

'I'm not your best friend any more, Paris Williams!'

Paris was squealing like a pig.

'*Ouch! You* were the one who said to tell because you didn't want Skippy to go home!'

Adam whirled the donkey faster. Fay yanked harder, pulling Paris along the shingle on her back.

'I hate you, Paris! You promised not to say anything to Adam on your rabbit's life.'

Skippy was running up and down, flapping his arms in distress.

Paris was screaming, 'Let go! Get *off* . . . OK-eeee . . . I *promise!*'

Fay let go. Adam let Twonk dangle by his tail for a few seconds, then put him away. Paris and Fay sat back to back, howling. Skippy squeezed between them and joined in. Adam didn't know what to do.

'Shh! Be quiet! *Stop it!*' his own voice was shaking now. 'Stop *crying!* You've got to go home!'

*

Apart from an occasional shuddering sob from the girls, the three of them walked back to Paris's house in silence.

'Paris isn't feeling very well, Mrs Williams,' Adam explained. 'She ate too much cheese round at our house.'

Her mother wasn't in the least sympathetic.

'Oh, Paris. That was greedy!'

She thanked Adam for bringing her back.

'Any time,' he said.

He didn't say a word to Fay until they got to the spinney. He'd been walking fast and Fay was out of breath trying to keep up with him. The suspense was unbearable. What would he do to her?

Suddenly, he stopped. He didn't turn round, he just stopped and looked straight ahead. Fay stood a few paces behind and stared at her shoes.

'He'll have to go back tomorrow now,' Adam said. 'And all because of you.'

Fay could feel tears prickling her eyes again.

'No, he won't. Paris won't say anything. She won't, I swear!'

'She will. Or *you* will. When were you going to do it? Tonight? *When*?'

He turned round and pushed her against a tree.

'You promised not to tell anyone, Fay. How could you? I'll never trust you again.'

'It's too big a secret!' she blurted. 'It's too big. We have to tell someone. It's not right.'

'He's going back tomorrow.'

Fay squared up to him.

'No! If you send Skippy back tomorrow, I'll tell Mum!'

Adam pulled the little donkey out of his pocket and held it up by the neck, but this time, it didn't have the desired effect.

'Go on then!' yelled Fay. 'Pull his head off if you want. I do *love* Twonk but not as much I love Skippy. And he loves me. You can't send him away. I'm telling!'

She held her breath and waited to see what Adam would do. To her surprise, he sat down on the path and put his head in his hands. His shoulders were heaving. Automatically, she knelt down to comfort him, but he pushed her away.

'I'm sorry, Adam. I'm sorry . . .'

He was inconsolable.

'You know what they did to ET!' he gulped. 'If I don't send him back tomorrow, they'll capture him and do experiments on him. It'll kill him. Is that what you want?'

Fay shook her head miserably.

'But I'll *miss* him!'

'You think I won't?' blurted Adam. 'You think I'm not really lonely? I've got nobody!'

He was an insignificant dot. He didn't belong on this planet any more than Skippy did. He wished he could go with him. Be his co-pilot. Better to be a misfit in Julutem than here.

'You've got me,' said Fay.

Adam shook his head.

'I don't want *you*. Everyone wants *you*.'

'No they don't. I'm sick of you saying that! Sonny makes you look after me and you don't want to, Dad can't because he's in the shop . . .'

'Mum wants you.'

'She doesn't, Adam! She makes me go to all these different things, pretending it's because she wants me to have everything she never had, but it isn't really. She does it to get rid of me!'

Adam had never thought of it like that before, but she was right! Apart from ferrying her from one lesson to the next, Mum spent no time with Fay at all.

'Fay, if Mum can't even be bothered to look after you, do you really think she'll want to look after Skippy?'

Fay frowned. Now he'd put it like that, she felt awful for even thinking about confiding in her mother. She'd have Skippy carted off to choir practice. He'd be lingering in the After-School Club. Banged up in bassoon lessons.

'OK. I won't tell Mum on one condition . . .'

'Skippy can't stay, Fay. How many more times?'

But that wasn't what she was going to say.

'I meant on the one condition you don't hate me for telling Paris Williams.'

Adam brushed the dirt off his trousers.

'I don't hate you, Fay.'

'You don't? So, you like me a little bit?'

Her voice broke when she said it. She gave him such a hopeful smile, he had to bite his lip. It made him hate himself more than he did already.

'Yeah, but it doesn't stop me being lonely. It's not your fault, Fay. I can't explain it.'

He didn't have to.

'You really miss Moses, don't you, Ad?'

He nodded. He couldn't speak. She gave him her hanky.

'Do you think he'll ever come back?'

He cleared his throat and regained his composure.

'I wish. The thing is, somewhere in Julutem, someone must be saying the same thing about Skippy. Someone's really missing him. I know how that feels. That's why he has to go.'

'Not to punish me?'

'No. That's not the reason.'

When they got back to Lurie's Motors, Fay tugged his hand and had one more try.

'I know Skippy can't stay, but please can we keep him one more day? Just *one* more?'

Adam noticed his mother's car parked outside. She was back from her retreat. He couldn't bring Fay home in tears.

'OK.'

'You promise?'

He nodded and they went inside.

Chapter Eight

Fay had a ballet exam in London the next day. She cornered Adam in his bedroom before she left. He'd just slipped a photo of himself into his backpack.

'You won't send Skippy back while I'm gone, will you?'

'No.'

She sighed with relief.

'Promise?'

'Go on. Mum's calling. You'll miss your train.'

'Wish me luck, Adam.'

'Luck.'

After she'd gone, he went straight down to The Black Hole on his bike and woke Skippy up.

'We've got a very busy morning,' he told him.

Despite what he'd said to Fay, she would never see Skippy again. He didn't feel good about it, but there it was; he couldn't put it off any longer. Skippy had run out of tablets. Paris Williams couldn't be trusted to keep her mouth shut and he wasn't sure his sister could either.

On a practical level, he'd never be able to look after Skippy once the school holidays had finished. It really was time he left.

Today, they would set the rocket up on the cliff. Adam was going to hide it under some gorse. When it was dark, he would creep out of the flat, cut through the back alley and make his way to the beach.

They would say their final goodbye on the cliff top. Skippy would start the ignition, Adam would cut the tethers and with an earth-shattering rumble, the rocket would zoom beyond the moon and carry its weary pilot home.

With a heavy heart, Adam loaded the nose cone onto the go-cart and strapped it in. Skippy frowned at him over a pot of fromage frais. Adam stopped what he was doing.

'Going to miss me, Skip?'

Skippy nodded.

'Me too,' Adam sighed. 'At least you've got mates back home. I haven't. Not now Moses has gone.'

'Moses,' said Skippy.

'My best friend,' Adam reminded him. 'My only friend, except for you.'

He pointed to the names they'd scratched into the cave wall.

'See this? He wrote it – Starflight Commander M. Shoderu – that was him.'

He gave Skippy his penknife.

'Write your name. It'll give me something to remember you by.'

Skippy put his head to one side, then carved an X. Then something that looked like an H, then an A, or was it just a triangle?

'S 'ave it!' he said.

'You want to have my penknife? Yeah, keep it. Why not? I couldn't think what present to get you. It'll be useful, too.'

Skippy tried to give him the knife back, but Adam insisted he kept it and slid it into his pocket.

'There . . . let's get on with it, then.'

He grabbed hold of the go-cart handle.

'You push, Skip. I'll pull.'

The nose cone was quite light. Between them, they dragged it up the cliff to the launch pad without a hitch. Adam had chosen the site with great care. The area had to be large enough to set everything up, but not too exposed. He'd decided on a wide platform covered with coarse grass, which jutted out to the left of the cliff path. It was obscured by a lip of overhanging rock, so no one could see them from above.

There was a sheer drop on to the shingle below, but now that Uncle Eugene had harnessed the power of Quinzone X, it was of no concern to Adam. This rocket was going up.

Putting his goalie gloves on to protect himself from the thorns, Adam hacked off some branches of gorse and arranged them over the nose cone to camouflage it. When he stood back, it had disappeared. No one would know it was there unless they fell over it.

They half-walked, half-rode the go-cart to the bottom of the cliff path and reloaded. This time, they had to carry the cockpit section. There was no fuel in the tank yet. It didn't seem too heavy at first, but by the time they got halfway up the cliff, the strain was beginning to show.

Just as they were turning a tight corner, Skippy skidded on some loose chalk, sank on to his knees and let go. With no one supporting the weight of the cart from behind, Adam was dragged backwards. He was sliding too fast to get a grip.

The go-cart was hurtling towards the edge of the cliff. Just as he thought it was going to drag him to his death, his right foot caught in a stirrup of thick root growing out of the path. Bracing himself, he hung onto the go-kart handle, making desperate head signals to Skippy.

'Get round the back of the cart . . . *quick I can't hold it.*'

With a typical lack of urgency, Skippy made his way to the opposite end of the go-cart and pushed against it with his back, one heel dangling dangerously in mid-air. Adam felt his breakfast rising into his throat. If he let go now, the cart, the cockpit and Skippy would go straight over the edge.

He leant back and pulled so hard, he thought the sinews in his neck would snap. Skippy gave a big push and the cart bounced back up the track.

'Keep *going*, Skip! Keep *going!*'

If they stopped, they'd slide back down. Adam scrambled madly up the steep slope until he was parallel with the launch pad, then he skewed the go-kart round so it couldn't roll back before collapsing in the long grass on his stomach.

When he finally raised his head and opened his eyes, he was staring straight into Skippy's, their noses almost touching. He was so close, it seemed like he only had one green eye in the middle of his forehead, brimming with tears.

'Adam . . .?' he said.

'What?'

Skippy crinkled up his face. He was struggling to say something, then he stopped. He was lost for words. Adam could feel the soft, fruit-flavoured haze of his breath against his own mouth.

'What is it, Skippy? Don't you want to go?'

Whatever it was he wanted to say, it was too big a secret.

'It's all right,' he whispered. 'It'll be all right. I don't want you to go either, but it's better this way. Your friends will be missing you.'

The tear fell. There was only one. Adam watched it fall into the grass and dissolve.

'Please be happy, Skip. I'm really glad you came, you know? I wish I knew why you did, but I don't suppose you're allowed to tell me, are you?'

He traced the yellow bruise on Skippy's brow where the blond boy had hit him with the pebble. The swelling had gone down now. His face had its own moonlike beauty. Would he ever come back? Adam wouldn't blame him if he didn't.

'Listen to me, Skip. When you go home, will you do me a favour? Tell them we're not all like the blond boy. I don't know if the human race is worth saving, but just tell them we're not all bad.'

Skippy didn't reply straight away. He sat up and looked far out to sea.

'Kam humbur familje,' he said.

The only word Adam understood was the last one. It sounded like family.

'You miss your family? You'll see them soon,' Adam reassured him. 'I bet they're a whole lot better than mine. They couldn't be worse.'

Sonny was coming home tonight. He was dreading it. It had been so relaxing, not having to think about having his head pulled off or being dangled out of a window.

'You never met Sonny, did you, Skip – my big brother? I was hoping he'd get killed in a fight, but I bet he hasn't.'

'Fay?' asked Skippy.

'Oh . . . Fay's at ballet. She said to say goodbye.'

Adam looked away. She would never understand that he wasn't doing this out of spite. He knew that, but there was nothing he could do. He walked over to the go-cart, dropped the front flap and tipped the cockpit section on to the grass. He cut some more gorse to cover it over.

'Nearly there now,' he said. 'Just two more loads and we can have a rest.'

Two more was too much. By the time they'd struggled to the top with the engine section and then the fin section, his head was pounding. Skippy looked positively ill. Adam was worried it was because he hadn't had his tablets today. He hoped he'd be fit enough to pilot the rocket.

'You'll feel better by tonight,' he said, helping Skippy into the cart. 'You're just exhausted in this heat. Even I'm knackered, and I'm used to the climatic conditions on Earth.'

He pushed him as far as he could down the cliff side. Where it was too steep for the cart, he had to make Skippy get out and walk. But he could hardly stand. Adam couldn't hold him up and handle the cart at the same time. Although it took twice as much effort, he had to park the go-cart to one side, carry Skippy down the tricky bits, then go back for it.

It was late afternoon by the time they arrived at The Black Hole. Adam's back was aching so much it hurt to stand up straight. He gave Skippy some water but he refused to eat, so Adam helped him on to the lilo and let him sleep.

Sleep wasn't an option for Adam. He still had to bolt the rocket together, pack it with provisions and fill the fuel tank. He was going to leave the nose cone off until Skippy was inside, so they could communicate up to the last minute.

He had a swig of water and pressed his fingers into his temples to try and relieve his pounding headache. Maybe it would help if he ate something. There was a banana in his backpack. He had been going to give it to Skippy for the journey, but decided it was a pretty stupid thing to take. Bananas didn't travel well. It would be brown mush by the time it got to Julutem.

He peeled it and made his way back up the cliff, swinging the fuel can.

*

The Harley Panhead Sonny had borrowed was parked outside Lurie's Motors. Adam's heart sank. He was shattered – all he wanted to do was go indoors, have some Disprin and go to sleep. Fat chance. The minute he walked in, it started.

'Look who it isn't? It's Dweeb!' Sonny announced. He had a large, purple gash across his forehead.

'Oh dear. Someone hit you with an axe,' muttered Adam. 'Did you feel it?'

Sonny grabbed him, lifted him up off the floor and held him upside down.

'I didn't *feel* it half as much as the other geezer. You should see the state of him. And we ripped his patch off.'

Adam let himself go floppy.

'*Fight*, Dweeb! What's the matter with you, you over-cooked bag of spaghetti.'

'Hi, Mum,' said Adam.

'You've been in five seconds and it's started already!' she snapped. 'Adam, get down and stop being silly.'

'I *can't* get down!' he insisted.

'Sonny, put your brother down. Now!'

'But he *likes* it, don't you, Dweeb? It's like being in outer space. Wheeeeee!'

Sonny began to whirl Adam round. His head knocked a framed wedding photo over, which smashed face down on the cabinet. His mother picked up her handbag and left.

'That's it! You can tell your dad I've gone round to Jocelyn's.'

Sonny threw Adam onto the sofa.

'Now you've gone and upset Karen. Now we'll have to make our own tea.'

He squashed Adam's nose with his oily thumb.

'If any girls ring up, you tell them I'm in the bath.'

Adam wanted to have a bath, but now there'd be no hot water. Sonny always used it all. He liked boiling in oil, he said. The phone rang. It was someone called Tina.

'Sonny's dead,' Adam told her.

The phone rang several times. Someone called Linda, then a Juliette, then two different Hannahs. When the phone rang again, it was Bonita.

'He's in prison,' Adam told her and slammed the receiver down.

Sonny came down with a towel round his waist. 'Who was that?'

'It was for me,' said Adam. 'It was Moses.'

He'd thought of ringing Moses, but he wasn't sure what time it would be in South Africa. He wished Moses would write. He said he would.

Sonny dropped his towel on the floor and stood in front of the mirror thrusting his pelvis.

'Bet you wish you had a butt like mine,' he said. 'Only you never will, because *you* are a different *species*.'

Adam put his fingers down his throat.

*

Skippy woke up in a sweat. He thought he heard gunshots. He lay there, shaking in the dark on the lilo, not sure whether it was day or night. He called softly for Adam. He often called for him, but sometimes he called for others.

'Giyshe? Dajë? Teze?'

They never came. He would wait and wait. After a while, someone would come with strange food – Adam or Fay – and he would forget about the others.

Right now, he was thirsty. Adam had left him an opened can of drink. He tried to reach it with his free hand, but knocked it on to the cave floor. It span, swirling froth which rapidly soaked away. Skippy reached out to grab the can with his other hand and found that he could – Adam had forgotten to strap him down.

That wasn't right. Skippy drank what was left of the lukewarm drink, put his hand back in the belt strap and held it closed. He didn't want Adam to be cross. Adam was his friend. Where was Fay?

'Fay?'

She wasn't there. Where was Adam?

'Adam!'

He spotted the backpack. Adam had left it in the cave. He wondered what was in it. Adam always opened it and gave him things from inside. Skippy limped over on his sore legs and undid the bag. Cake. Meat in a jar. Water in a bottle. Clothing. What was this? He held it close to his eyes. It was the photo.

'Adam,' he murmured.

He wanted to be with Adam. He remembered now. They'd taken the rocket to the top of the cliff. Up and down. Up and down. Adam was at the top of the cliff with the rocket. Skippy wanted to sit in the cockpit. He rolled back the driftwood and tiptoed across the shingle in his bare feet.

It was dusk. The moon and the moths were out. All was quiet, except for the *shhh* of the sea and the babble of seagulls settling down for the night. Skippy made his way slowly up the cliff path, planting his toes in the powdery scuff marks Adam's shoes had made earlier.

He came to the place where the go-cart had skidded near the edge of the cliff and sat there for a while, swinging his legs, watching the waves gallop along the horizon – white horses! The sea wasn't like the sea where he lived. It was a different colour. He drew round Adam's moon with his finger. He had a moon like that at home.

Skippy made his way further up the cliff path with the photo of Adam in his hand. He'd had a picture of his family when he arrived, but it had gone. He'd had some papers too. He shouldn't have lost them. They were important. Giyshe would be angry.

He almost missed the turning which led to the launch pad, but then he remembered Adam had cut a cross in a big chalky stone. There was the stone. There was the cross. He crawled through the grass to where the rocket lay hidden under the gorse.

No Adam.

It hurt pulling the gorse away. It made his hands bleed, but it didn't stop him. He would sit in the rocket and wait for Adam. He would come soon.

The rocket was all put together, except for the nose cone. Skippy slid into the cockpit and settled down in the seat. Adam had shown him the controls many times. That was the ignition. He pressed it and the red light came on. He pushed the starter button. The engine began to throb. At first, it made a low growl. Skippy could feel the vibrations buzzing through his body.

Suddenly, a dog burst into the clearing. It was barking, jumping up at him. Skippy panicked. He tried to engage the clutch. He opened the throttle wide, wider still, to get away. The rocket began to shake violently, the untethered ropes creeping along behind it as it inched forward. As the whine of the motor rose to a scream, Skippy felt a hand on his shoulder.

'Adam?'

No! A woman staring at him, wide-eyed, dog lead in her hand, shouting! Why?

He couldn't hear over the noise of the engine. Her mouth was opening and shutting like a fish. Red-faced, frowning, trying to pull him out. Scared! Being attacked! Please, no more boys with stones. Men with guns. He kicked out.

'*Ndih'me!*'

Teeth sank into soft flesh. He could taste the salt. His head was swimming – little black dots swimming over his eyes. He was slipping out of the rocket, being dragged along on his back, sliding into darkness. Dog barking, barking, barking. A big flash, he can see it even through his closed eyelids.

BOOM!

A massive explosion, like a bomb – so loud, it made the flat over Lurie's Motors shake.

'Christ!'

Chas spat out his tinned spaghetti.

'What the hell was that?'

Everybody rolled their eyes.

'Uncle Eugene?' they groaned.

Chapter Nine

As the fire brigade removed the melted remains of the rocket, Skippy was on his way to hospital in an ambulance. He wasn't aware of the journey, because he'd had a seizure. When he woke up, he was lying on a narrow bed in a small room by himself. He couldn't work out where he was or how he got there. He called for Adam.

A woman came and spoke to him softly, but he didn't understand what she was saying. She was waving his empty bottle of pills and asking questions. He recognized some of the words. Adam used them, but he couldn't remember how to answer in Adam's language.

The nurse took his temperature, patted his arm and left. He rolled over and went back to sleep. The next time he woke, he was surrounded by people in white coats. At first, he thought they were angels. There was an old man with glasses and a clipboard who spoke sternly:

'May we examine you?'

Skippy didn't know what was being asked of him. He nodded and rocked. The man took out a tape measure and held it around Skippy's head.

'Note the circumference,' he said. 'It is microcephalic – noticeably small due to the failure of brain growth. Note also the short eye openings with epicanthic folds, the sunken nasal bridge.'

He pointed to the area under Skippy's nose with his pen.

'Observe the absence of a philtrum. There is no perceptible nose groove, an almost absent upper lip. Any ideas what these features might indicate?'

'Maybe he's a Martian?' someone quipped.

Some of the students giggled. Others shook their heads. The old man lost his temper.

'Come on, *examine* him! Don't stand there cracking stupid jokes. You're not in the student bar now, you're in a teaching hospital.'

One of the young women started to uncurl Skippy's fingers.

'There's a shortening of the metacarpal bones leading to the fourth and fifth finger, sir. And a single transverse crease on the palm?'

He thought she wanted to hold his hand, but she pulled away.

'That's more like it,' the old man smiled. 'It's called a Simian Crease.'

He held Skippy's hand up and spread the fingers open.

'The fine motor skills are impaired, there is poor hand/eye co-ordination. I'm looking for a syndrome. Any ideas? Quickly!'

He snapped his fingers. The others fell upon Skippy, peeling back his lips, peering in his mouth, lifting up his gown. Running their hands over his curved, bare back.

'Scoliosis of the spine, sir.'

They were turning him over this way, that way.

'He has a heart murmur.'

They explored him with inexperienced, gloved hands. He was too weak to fight them off. They lifted him under the armpits, undid his gown and stood him naked in the middle of the room. They waited with folded arms.

'Dua Giyshe!' he wailed.

Nobody understood.

'Speech defects are common, partly caused by the mal-alignment of the teeth and also retardation. Pay attention to his gait – watch how he walks.'

Skippy flapped his arms and tottered round in a circle. They wrote things down. They wouldn't hold him when he clung to their knees. Still no one could guess what was wrong with him.

'Patients suffering from this affliction crave physical attention. They are fearless, friendly to total strangers. While that may seem charming in a child, you can imagine the problems it causes when they are adults. They cannot learn from their mistakes. Thus, they become criminals, misfits . . . outcasts.'

A student put his hand up, 'What about special education, sir?'

The old man shook his head.

'Special education is of no use whatsoever, Johnson. The child has Fetal Alcohol Syndrome. Its brain is pickled. You can't un-pickle a brain any more than you can un-pickle a walnut. To put it in a nutshell.'

He paused, smiling at his own joke while they fumbled for their notebooks.

'Take this down. Fetal Alcohol Syndrome is the total sum of damage done to a foetus before birth. It is entirely due to its mother drinking alcohol during pregnancy.'

There was a flicker of sympathy in his expression as he cast a critical eye over Skippy.

'His mother must have had a skin full. He's a particularly sorry specimen.'

'Surely if we *educated* the mothers, sir?'

It was Johnson again. The consultant blinked rapidly with thinly disguised irritation.

'Do you want to be a social worker or a doctor?' he barked. 'Do hurry up and decide! While you're faffing around educating someone's mother, I've got a hospital full of sick people you might actually be able to help.'

The nurse returned. One of the cleaning staff who came from the Balkans had managed to translate the words on Skippy's medicine bottle. The tablets were Dilantin, used to control fits.

'The directions were written in Shquip,' explained the nurse. 'This little boy is Albanian, I should think.'

[104]

Skippy was sitting on the floor. She crouched down and spoke to him.

'Shquip?' she asked.

He shook his head enthusiastically.

'Squeep!'

'He's denying it, nurse,' the doctor scoffed. 'I'm afraid you won't get much sense out of him.'

She gave him a terse look.

'He's *agreeing* with me. Albanians shake their heads when they mean Yes.'

The doctor was unapologetic. He muttered something under his breath and filed out with his students.

The nurse put Skippy's gown back on and helped him into bed. He put his arms round her and she sat with him for as long as he needed, even though she was far too busy.

*

Adam stood up, stretched and announced he was going to have an early night.

'Why?' asked Fay. 'It's not even my bedtime. Mum's not back from Aunty Jocelyn's yet.'

'I'm bored stiff listening to him going on and on about Knebworth.'

Adam pointed at Sonny, who was picking his toenails in a chair. Sonny threw his socks at him.

'You're so jealous, man. I burnt up the road with my devoted disciples, did major battle and generally had a good crack – and you? You pulled the short straw. You looked after Fay.'

'I'm not a short straw!' Fay protested. 'I'm Adam's friend now.'

'You're the only one,' Sonny sniggered. 'Dweeb is Billy No-Mates. He has to hang around with little girls. Nothing against you, Faybee. Karen said you did a great ballet exam.'

'Did she? Did she really? Shall I show you what I did, Sonny? I had my white tutu on, and my white ballet shoes and I started off like this . . . are you watching?'

Fay stood in the middle of the room in first position. One word of flattery from Sonny and she danced to his tune. She did a few fairy steps then stuck her leg behind her ear. Adam walked out in disgust.

He didn't feel so guilty about breaking his promise now. Fay didn't worship him above her other friends after all. All right, she was no Moses, but it gave him a buzz, thinking he was special to her. He'd kidded himself. She liked everyone. Anyone. Even Sonny.

He went to his room, locked the door and drew his curtains. He sat down at his desk, took out a biro and tore a sheet of lined paper out of his old homework book.

Dear Moses

I hope you are having a good time and have made new friends.

He crossed it out and started again. He hated the thought of Moses making new friends. He hoped he was as lonely as he was, then maybe he'd come back.

Dear Starflight Commander Shoderu

By the time you get this letter, I will have done something beyond your wildest dreams. Remember when we talked about the ocean on Europa (it's actually called Julutem) and remember you said there had to be intelligent life there? Well, guess what, Commander? You were right . . .

The letter went on for five pages. He told Moses everything; all about finding the washed-up rocket, how he'd found Skippy in the rock pool, beaten up the blond boy and how he'd helped to invent Quinzone X. He got quite carried away, his deeds becoming more heroic and exaggerated with every line. When he'd finished, he drew Skippy's portrait on a separate piece of paper and put it in the envelope.

I'd have sent you a photo of him but couldn't risk having it developed in case the man in the chemists saw it and grassed me up.

He enclosed Uncle Eugene's drawings too.

I want you to keep these blueprints of the rocket safe for me . You are the only person I can trust. They'll never think to look for them in South Africa. If it all goes wrong tonight and the authorities search my room, I'm going to deny everything. I don't want NASA to find any evidence, for Skippy's sake.

He'd signed the letter Captain Lurie and added a PS.

Please destroy this letter as soon as you've read it.

And a PPS.

Send me a postcard.

He stuck three first-class stamps on the envelope. It seemed rather a lot, but the envelope was heavy and it had to get to Cape Town. He'd post it tonight before he went to fetch Skippy.

He looked at his watch. It was nine o'clock. He had three hours to kill before the launch. All the preparations had been done. The fuel tank was filled, the Quinzone X had been carefully measured out and added. He'd even arranged a pulley with two ropes to raise the rocket to the right angle once the pilot was inside.

His stomach turned over. He suddenly remembered he'd left Skippy's hand unstrapped! What if he'd wandered off?

He relaxed – Skippy was exhausted after carrying all the parts up the cliff top. He'd still be sound asleep. Adam was tired too. He ached all over. He set the alarm on his watch for eleven-thirty, climbed into bed with all his clothes on and shut his eyes.

The cleaning woman from the Balkans sat on the edge of Skippy's hospital bed, held his hand and asked him something in Albanian.

'He say his name is Xhavit,' she told the nurse. 'I ask where he's from – Prej nag vjen? Tirana? Peza? Girokastra?'

He wouldn't tell her.

'Dua Adam, julutem,' he pleaded.

The nurse looked puzzled. 'What does he want?'

'He saying he want Adam, please. *Julutem* mean the same as *please* in English.'

She asked if she could give Skippy a mint from her overall pocket. The nurse nodded and listened as the cleaner continued her questioning.

After sucking the mint slowly, Skippy told her Adam was on top of the cliff and that he lived in a *shpelle*.

'In a cave?'

'Po.'

The cleaning woman translated. 'He say yes, he been living in a cave.'

'What, all by himself?'

'No, he had an auntie and uncle and two cousins but when he woke up, they had gone,' the cleaner whispered to the nurse behind her hand.

'Now we getting somewhere. He is asylum seeker, I think. Probably come over on the boat, you know? He may be *jetim* – an orphan?'

She put her arm round Skippy and asked him about his mother.

'Nene Vdi kur,' he told her.

'Mother is dead. Giyshe – grandma – looked after him. She had hidden him in the tomato lorry with Teze and Daje and his cousins. They were to look after him. They were to stay with friends in Britain.'

'With Adam?'

'No, other friends. Friends of his uncle. But the lorry stopped in the dark and made them all get out. They were lost. They had to sleep on the beach. When he woke, his family had gone.' The cleaner clicked her tongue in disgust.

'They abandoned him! What will happen to him now?'

At eleven o'clock that night, Skippy was declared fit enough to travel. He was put in an unmarked vehicle and taken to a disused military camp. There he waited to be processed with all the other aliens who had come in search of a saviour and fallen into the hands of Barbarians.

He called for Adam in his sleep.

Chapter Ten

Something woke Adam seconds before his alarm went off. He sat up with a start and looked at his watch. Good – he was ahead of schedule. He grabbed the letter he'd written to Moses and stuffed it in his pocket.

He listened at his door to make sure no one was about. Sonny had gone to bed around ten. Adam could hear him snoring through the thin walls. He wasn't likely to wake in a hurry, he hadn't slept in a bed for days. He'd refused to take a sleeping bag to Knebworth.

'The Outcasts sleep where they fall!' he'd insisted.

'Let's hope you fall in the river,' Adam had replied.

His mother's car wasn't back, which meant she was still at Jocelyn's. It was Sunday, so Chas would have nodded off in front of the telly, surrounded by lager cans. He should be able to sneak out unnoticed. He tiptoed into the hall.

'Hey! Where are you going?'

Adam's heart skipped a beat.

'Go back to bed, Fay.'

She stood there in her pink nightie, arms folded, blocking his way.

'No *way*,' she hissed. 'I know where you're going! You're going to send Skippy back, aren't you? . . . *aren't you*!'

He couldn't deny it. Fay's lower lip trembled.

'You weren't even going to tell me! You promised!'

Her voice was starting to rise. She was about to ruin every-thing. Adam smiled sweetly and coaxed her back into his room.

'OK, OK. Come on . . . come?'

For a moment, he fooled Fay into thinking something good was going to happen. Maybe he was going to let her come with him at least, and say goodbye to Skippy. The second she was out of earshot, he clapped his hand over her mouth and pulled her against him.

'Don't you dare screw this up for me, Fay. I'll never speak to you again. *Never*.'

He could feel her heart fluttering against her ribcage. He squeezed hard. That was odd, his hand felt wet. She was *licking* it! He opened his fingers in revulsion.

'Ugh!'

She bit his thumb until it crunched and stamped down hard on his instep. He was in agony. He wanted to sit down and nurse his foot, but she was getting away. He tried to grab her by the arm. Missed! She karate-chopped him on the shoulder and sprang back, glowering.

'If you let Skippy go, I'll tell Sonny you stole his bike!'

They stared at each other in silence, then she repeated the threat.

'I'll tell Sonny! I mean it.'

Without warning, Adam rugby tackled her round the knees. She looked so startled, he laughed, but as she fell back, she banged her head on the desk and crumpled. He hadn't meant that to happen. He knelt down and tried to help her up.

'Rub it hard. Come on, it's only a bump.'

He tried to jolly her along so she wouldn't cry. It was too late. She sat up, felt her scalp and looked at her fingers. They were smeared with blood. She opened her mouth slowly, silently, building up to a scream.

'No, Fay. Don't yell. Don't! For Skippy's sake?'

It was too late. She wasn't listening. She threw back her head and shrieked.

'*Son-neeeeeeeeee!*'

Adam backed out of the room.

'*Da-deeeeeeeeee!*'

Chas stirred in his chair. Adam ducked into the kitchen. He

could hear Sonny's feet landing on the floor as he swung himself out of bed. He was muttering grumpily to Fay.

'Whassup? I was asleep.'

Then he saw the blood.

'Jeez! What happened . . . ?'

Adam didn't catch the rest. He could hear Fay talking in
sobs, but the words were muffled as if she had her head
pressed into Sonny's shoulder. He tiptoed out of the kitchen
towards the front door. He'd almost got there when he heard
a key rattle in the lock. Mum was home!

He skidded back into the kitchen and hid behind the boiler.
His mother was humming to herself. She broke off and went
into the front room.

'Chas? Chas! Turn the volume down!'

He'd fallen asleep again. She tutted and snapped the televi-
sion off. Adam prayed she wouldn't come into the kitchen. It
was the least of his problems.

'*He did what?*'

Fay had told Sonny about the bike. He was booting doors
open. Adam could hear them smacking against the walls. His
stomach went into a tight knot.

'*Where is he? I'm going to kill him.*'

His mother came into the hall, looking confused.

'Do you have to shout?'

Sonny pushed past her and kicked the bathroom door off
its hinges.

'Are you in there, Dweeb?'

Now Chas was awake. He flew out of his chair and grabbed
hold of Sonny in a vain attempt to stop him wrecking the place.

'Sonny, pack it in! What's your problem?'

Sonny shook him off.

'Get *off*! He nicked my *motorbike*! He nicked my *bike*! Where
is he?'

'Mummy, I'm bleeding!' whimpered Fay.

While his parents comforted Fay, Adam took a deep breath
and charged for the front door. Sonny bared his teeth and

advanced on him, fists clenched.

'Dweeb? *Come here!*'

Adam pelted down the iron staircase and jumped on to his waiting pushbike. Sonny leant over the top of the stairs with Chas hanging on to his arm.

'I'm gonna have you! I'm gonna crucify you . . .'

The door slammed. Chas must have dragged him back inside. Adam could hear them arguing through the open window. Fay was crying. A pane of glass smashed.

He pedalled faster. Down the alleyway. Through the Spinney.

'Keep going. Keep going. It'll be all right,' he told himself.

In the back of his mind, he felt it would be. Fay didn't know where the launch pad was. Even if Sonny followed, it would take him a while to find it. There would be enough time to winch the rocket up and launch it. He and Skippy would just have to say a short goodbye.

Using his feet as brakes, he stuffed his letter to Moses into the postbox and sped down the hill. He was almost at the beach. No one was following. He was going to get away with this!

He skidded on to the shingle, threw his bike down and ran up to The Black Hole. The driftwood wasn't in the entrance. Why not? He thought he'd replaced it. Damn! He went inside and shone his torch around the cave. He was so out of breath, he could hardly speak.

'Skip?'

Skippy wasn't on the lilo. The belt lay undone on the pillow . . . he'd gone.

'Oh, no . . . Oh no . . .'

Adam cursed himself for not strapping him in. Skippy had gone off without his shoes. What now . . . what *now*?

Adam grabbed his backpack and went outside. He swung his torch round, searching wildly for signs along the beach. Nothing. Nobody! What if he'd drowned? He cupped his hands to his mouth and called out.

'Skip . . . eee?'

No answer. He threw his torch down in frustration and went into a crouch, hugging his knees. The torch bounced off a stone and landed sideways in a tussock of grass. Adam looked up. The beam was illuminating a long footprint in the chalk dust at the bottom of the cliff.

Adam picked up the torch and waved it along the path. There were more footprints. Skippy must have gone up the cliff! Of *course* he had. He knew tonight was the night! Adam had told him often enough. Take-off was meant to be at midnight. Adam looked at his watch. He was late. Skippy would be waiting for him in the cockpit. Spurred on by this thought, he began to climb.

'Hang on. Don't you go without me, Skippy!'

He'd only been climbing for a few minutes when he heard an ominous rumbling sound. Motorbike engines. Not one, but two. They were getting louder. He ducked down.

'I can see you, Dwweeeeeeb!' bellowed Sonny. 'You can run but you can't hide!'

His mother was on the back of the bike. Closing up at the rear was Chas. Fay had her arms wrapped round him, riding pillion in her nightie.

'I see him!' she screeched. 'There he is! I see him!'

Adam scrambled higher, his nails worn down to the skin on the chalky path. Sonny was prowling around at the bottom of the cliff, making the engine growl. Adam heard the tone change . . .

He was riding the bike up! It was whining and spitting stones out from under its wheels.

'*I'm coming to get you, Dweeb!*'

Adam stood high above him on a ledge. He was being hunted. Instinctively, he felt an overwhelming urge to attack the leader of the pack. He picked up a rock, lifted it above his head and hurled it as hard as he could at Sonny. It knocked his front wheel out of line.

Sonny wrestled with the bike for a fraction of a second, revved the engine like an angry wasp and drove it up in furious spurts, throwing his passenger around like a puppet. She was screaming.

'Sonny, slow down ! Please – you're going to kill us!'

'I'm going to kill *him*!'

Adam threw himself round the corner and staggered along the path, his lungs sucked dry.

'Hold on, Skippy, I'm coming!'

Sonny was drifting closer and closer on a cloud of carbon monoxide. Adam stumbled and wrenched his ankle. He tried to stand but couldn't put any pressure on his foot. He'd had it. They would catch him.

'Go away! Leave me *alone*!'

Suddenly, Sonny's engine stalled. Adam put his hands together and prayed out loud:

'Thank you, thank you, thank you.'

He crawled the last few metres to the chalk stone with the cross and dived off the path into the long grass that concealed the launch pad. He sat up and wiped the sweat from his eyes.

The rocket had gone. There was nothing left but a scorched circle in the bare earth. He looked up at the stars. Far away, he could see a glittering trail of fire speeding through the cosmos towards the planet of Julutem. Adam leapt into the air.

'*Haaaaaaaaaaaaah . . . he made it! He made it!*'

A motorbike throbbed at his heels. He laughed out loud. There was no reason to run any more. Somewhere out there, the citizens of Europa would praise his name and tell their children that Adam Lurie was good and kind and merciful beyond measure. They would believe in him.

He adjusted the radio on his invisible space helmet.

'This is Captain Lurie to Starflight Commander Shoderu. Mission accomplished. Over.'

Sonny could do what he liked to him now.